NO LO
ANY
RANGEV

D0032275

SEASONS
of the
MOON

NO LONGER PROPERTY OF
ANYTHINK LIBRARIES/
RANGEVIEW LIBRARY DISTRICT

SEASONS
of the
MOON

JULIEN ARANDA
TRANSLATED BY ROLAND GLASSER

This is a work of fiction. Names, characters, organizations, places, events, and incidents are either products of the author's imagination or are used fictitiously. Any resemblance to actual persons, living or dead, or actual events is purely coincidental.

Text copyright © 2014 Julien Aranda
Translation copyright © 2017 Roland Glasser
All rights reserved.

No part of this book may be reproduced, or stored in a retrieval system, or transmitted in any form or by any means, electronic, mechanical, photocopying, recording, or otherwise, without express written permission of the publisher.

Previously published as *Le sourire du clair de lune* by the author via the Kindle Direct Publishing Platform in France in 2014. Translated from French by Roland Glasser. First published in English by AmazonCrossing in 2017.

Published by AmazonCrossing, Seattle

www.apub.com

Amazon, the Amazon logo, and AmazonCrossing are trademarks of Amazon.com, Inc., or its affiliates.

ISBN-13: 9781542047777
ISBN-10: 1542047773

Cover design by Shasti O'Leary Soudant

Printed in the United States of America

To Élodie, to my parents, to my grandfather, to my family, and to my friends.

Kerassel, Morbihan, 1992

I was resting on my bed one evening when the doorbell rang. It gave me a bit of a shock, since I wasn't expecting anyone. My bedside clock said *8:30 p.m.* I got up in the half-light and peered out the window. A brown-haired man, around forty years old, was standing on my doorstep in a spotless suit. He didn't look like anyone I knew. *Must be a salesman,* I thought. Throwing on a jacket, I went to open the door and found myself facing a beaming smile.

"Good day, Mr. Vertune," said the man, in a Spanish accent.

"Hello. Can I help you?"

"Yes," he replied, looking me straight in the eye. "I want to thank you."

"What do you mean?"

"Thank you with all my heart," he said, bursting into tears.

NEW MOON

1

There's no such thing as chance in life. Except for life itself. One day my father glimpsed my mother. Or maybe it was the other way around—it doesn't matter. They met and there was a magic spark. It was love, or at least that's what it said on the document they signed in front of the village mayor. My story begins with their meeting, although the key moment was really that of my birth. An optimist would say that I was born in early summer. A pessimist would say late June. But one thing everyone agreed upon was the heat wave. For years afterward, old folk would regale anyone who'd care to listen with dramatic tales of the impact on their crops, their words heavy with the bitterness and resentment of those who have suffered, those whom nature did not spare. I came into the world slap-bang in the middle of this solar frenzy, having judged the climate favorable to make my way down the birth canal. Birth is to life what boredom is to imagination: one is not possible without the other. My mother felt her first contractions in the garden of the family farm, as she bent over the soil, picking the sun-gorged vegetables. Maternity leave had yet to be invented. Pregnant or not, women were at the service of their families. There was no question of taking time off. Clutching her belly, on her knees, my mother sent for the doctor and the village priest, who barely had time to gather their instruments, mount their bicycles, and furiously pedal the two miles to our farm. My father had also been informed but considered it insufficient reason to abandon work. I was merely his fourth child, after all. Doubtless it sickened him to see the bloody heads of his brats emerge from between his wife's thighs. Nature at work has no beauty but that which we give it, and my father was no artist in that regard. He preferred the solitude of his fields to the plaintive cries of his son. Farming was his life. The rest was unimportant.

◆　◆　◆

The priest and the doctor arrived at the same time. They leaned their bicycles against the garden fence.

"Good day, Doctor. How are you?" asked the priest, his voice full of that warmth one so often finds in men of faith.

"I am well, thank you," replied the doctor coldly.

"We don't often see you at mass on Sundays."

"That's because I don't like the taste of the wafers."

"If that's all it is, you are not obliged to swallow them!" joked the man of the cloth.

The doctor, put out by the priest's repartee, shrugged his shoulders. The holy man lowered his head, disappointed at having failed yet again to establish a dialogue with the doctor. All his attempts had been in vain, despite his commitment to Catholic tradition. His faith in humanity had not wavered—quite the contrary—but the doctor certainly didn't make life easy for him. The priest had to contend with that lack of open-mindedness that men of science sometimes have regarding spiritual matters: the barely masked intolerance that seems to make geniuses of them, holders of an age-old secret that ordinary people cannot even begin to glimpse, let alone understand, so ignorant are they. He took a chance every time he saw the doctor, just in case, but he never succeeded. The truth was that one of them considered procreation to be God's masterpiece, while the other saw it as a mere fact of life related

4

to the survival of the species. It was a major difference of opinion. I was not yet born, and already a paradox of life had me in its clutches. My umbilical cord had barely been severed, and already my body was buffeted between the doctor's instruments and the priest's holy water.

"Let me baptize him," the priest insisted.

"Hang on a second so I can check that his heart is beating properly!"

"Thank you, Lord, for this gift full of grace . . ."

"For heaven's sake, will you shut up, I can't hear a thing!" declared the doctor.

"I'm sorry, but I must proceed with the traditional rites of my church."

"To hell with your rites, let me do my work!"

The priest blanched at such a blasphemy.

The doctor passed his stethoscope across every part of my body; palpated my genitals; examined my pupils, my ears, my scalp, my fingers, and my feet. He tested my reflexes with a series of increasingly forbidding instruments. His medical ritual went on so long that my mother began to doubt its usefulness. She wondered whether all this fuss wasn't intended purely to infuriate the priest, who was so anxious to baptize my newborn body. Finally the doctor completed his meticulous examination.

"All is well, madam. Your son is in very good health."

"Thank you."

Turning to the priest, standing just behind him, he remarked scornfully, "He's yours now. Bless him with your nonsense!"

The priest gently picked me up and plunged my head into the holy water. He recited a few words of Latin before wrapping me in a towel. Some scientists affirm that on the day of our birth, our brain draws its own conclusions as to this strange masquerade that is life. These thoughts affect our existence for the rest of our days, as if attached to our heads by long strings.

Unfortunately, few people remember the day of their birth. The details of mine were related to me a few years later by one of my older brothers. He told me that as soon as each man grabbed me, my little brow furrowed and I howled inconsolably. I was already pining for my cozy nook deep in the maternal belly, where it all began, where nothing mattered, where all was silence and repose. But devious despair had gathered me as I exited the vagina. Nothing good awaited me out there. Or if there was any goodness, I would have to strive to unearth it. Perhaps that was my destiny. Perhaps the leitmotif of my life was determined the moment daylight tore into my retina: smooth out sharp corners, calm conflicts, understand rather than impose, love rather than hate.

Then, when the priest placed me in my mother's arms, my yelling ceased, as despair's spring suddenly ran dry. I somehow understood that my mother was my ally, my light in the darkness. Even then, a woman's presence gave me a pleasant feeling, different from that of men. But the true miracle of birth occurred next—not in the literal sense, the mechanics and blood of it, but the metaphorical, spiritual one. I cracked a wide smile, an offering to my mother, who was both moved and relieved to be separated from a part of herself. At that precise moment, a piece of theater was playing out in my unconscious, its protagonists serving up a spectacle bursting with conclusions. The first: beware of men and their unhealthy thirst for power. Second: if you must suffer, at least keep smiling while you do so; it costs nothing, as they say in the countryside. Third: live intensely and never seek refuge behind excuses you only half believe. A glow appeared in my eyes then, my pupils shimmering like a torch in the night.

2

On that hot summer day of June 26, 1929, I offered myself to life in all my nakedness: I was physically, intellectually, and emotionally raw. My mother took me in her arms and kissed me at length, and I snuggled against her, a fragile little animal, reliant on her care and affection. The priest observed the scene, a soft smile playing across his face. As for the doctor, he packed his instruments away in his bag without paying us any attention. He seemed in a hurry to leave the room.

"What will this little boy be called?" the man of the church asked my mother.

"Paul," she replied.

"That's a lovely name. Paul was the thirteenth apostle, according to the Catholic tradition. He was thought to be different from the others: sensitive, a poet and a dreamer, 'the apostle to the Gentiles.' Your son will wear his name well. I sense that he too is different."

"In what way?" the doctor interrupted. "He has a heart, two legs, two arms, two feet, two hands, a head! There is nothing as ordinary as a newborn, madam, with all due respect."

"I was speaking not of his corporeal envelope, Doctor, but what lies inside."

"Inside? There are guts, viscera, miles of veins through which a reddish liquid flows, bones to keep everything in place, nerves to make him move, muscles to help him carry wheat in the fields so he can feed his family, ligaments and tendons that will wear out with age, cells full of water—so much water, nothing but water everywhere—and, finally, a brain to give him a sense of priorities, of reality. That's what's inside this boy, Reverend, not a fiction that nobody can prove! Now excuse me, but I must go. I have other patients waiting for me to attend to their sick bodies, and it's not with a load of nonsense that I'll be treating what ails them. Goodbye, madam. Come see me regularly so that I may check on the good health of your child."

"Goodbye, Doctor," said the priest, disillusioned but never resentful.

The doctor hurried off, his bag hanging from his arm, then suddenly halted in the doorway and turned around.

"And I . . . My congratulations, madam, that's a lovely baby you have there," he uttered hesitantly before leaving.

My brother told me how the priest gave a slight smile as he congratulated my mother again before also leaving. He walked along the farm wall to his rusty old bicycle, mounted it, and slowly rode away, humming a hymn full of hope, its pleasant melody filling the country lane like a trail of human kindness put to good use, the sense of a duty properly accomplished. Then he disappeared from view.

When my father returned to the farm that evening, he stopped to peer at me. His face bore no emotion except the fatigue of a man exhausted by work.

"He doesn't look like me," he declared indifferently.

"Really? I think he has your eyes and lips," my mother replied.

"He looks like a wimp."

"It's a bit soon to tell."

"As long as he can help in the fields, that's all I care about."

Once he had satisfied his curiosity, he turned from the crib and went to tend to the animals. I represented nothing in his eyes but another mouth to feed and two more arms to help him harvest his fields. No more, no less. My destiny was already sealed in stone. I would follow my begetter's path in every detail, sowing the fertile earth with fistfuls of seed, bending to reap the golden stalks. In his mind there was no other path imaginable, no other way possible, no magic capable of supplanting the cruel reality of our country life. Fortune-tellers wouldn't be able to hustle me as they read my palm at the village fête; there would be nothing for them to remark upon, just a long, straight life line that met the demands of my progenitor.

My father was a mysterious man I never really knew. His features, betraying no emotion—not even a hint—never conveyed any sort of love for me. His eyes reflected an abyssal emptiness, a bottomless well that had filled with desolation when he was only a little boy, soaking deep into the surrounding rock. But the well's structure remained firm, unaffected by the stagnating putrefaction. His extreme coldness frightened me, as did his lack of humanity. A wall of incomprehension rose between us. I possessed all the emotion he lacked. Not to mention my enthusiasm, in overwhelming contrast to his gloomy, blinkered view of existence. We never became close. What did my mother love about such a stern man? I was unable to unravel the mystery of this paradoxical union, for the ways of love are, like those of the Lord, impenetrable.

Mama was the exact opposite of her husband. A fervent Catholic who attended mass every Sunday, she praised the glory of God while singing out of tune. Her attractive physique seemed unaffected by a series of pregnancies and a litany of household chores. Her body remained slender, soft, and childlike. Our physique often reflects our character. Open-minded, affectionate people appear younger, and those with closed minds and hearts, older, as if some interplay between our organs could inexorably curb our destiny. My mother loved me with all her might, with all her being, and she protected me from her husband's authority as best she could. She comforted me through the ups and downs of life with a courage my father sorely lacked.

3

My first years were punctuated by the mooing of cows, the smell of hay, the scent of raspberry bushes in the garden, and the salty spray of the sea lapping at the Brittany coastline a few hundred yards from our house. It was a carefree time, a golden age where the pleasure of experimentation was my sole concern, where I could appreciate life without thinking about tomorrow. I learned to talk, walk, and run full tilt through the varied landscapes of the Gulf of Morbihan. My three brothers, Jacques, Guy, and Pierre, introduced me to this environment where everything astonished me, be it insects, plants, shellfish, crustaceans, wheat fields, or the roads along which cars passed, their engines throbbing.

"Paul, look, a glowworm!" cried Jacques every time he spied one of the strange beetles that bathed the undergrowth with its pale light.

"Glooooowworm!" I shouted in wonder, emphasizing the *o* to such an extent that the word was soon no more than a shadow of itself.

I approached the insect, intrigued, believing it to have come from the era of the dinosaurs, devoting the same metaphysical worship to the beetle as the Incas did to the sun. I was fascinated by its world, a world of silence and rustling. A child's imagination is unspoiled, yet to be short-circuited by pernicious thoughts to come. No adult worships an insect, except perhaps an entomologist. I picked up the creature with infinite care and admired its delicate, soothing, greenish light.

Occasionally this light would extinguish for no apparent reason, and I would put it back, feeling guilty at having disrupted its luminous peace. Jacques always understood my disappointment and wrapped his arms around me. He was a great guy in those days.

◆ ◆ ◆

Sometimes, when my parents' backs were turned, I went out to our garden and explored the scattered apple orchard. I would sit in the shade of those huge trees, which every now and then would release a ripe fruit that made me jump as it hit the ground. I could spend hours with my eyes fixed on the sharply delineated leaves as they danced in the breeze, hypnotized by this aerial ballet. Often one would detach from its branch and glide above my head, twisting in the gusts of wind, twirling through empty space to land, rustling on the ground. Tiny insects streaked back and forth across the bark, winding their way around the branches without making a sound despite the millions of feet striking the wood. I would stretch out on the ground and admire the sky for hours, marveling at that bright blue stretching as far as the eye could see, or, when night fell, the dark cloak pricked with points of light. But something else up there intrigued me: a kind of luminous pebble perched in the black void. I would scrutinize it with concern, not understanding what it was doing there. Sometimes I would glimpse it overhead during the day, yet paler, more subdued. Its shape was always changing, from a crescent to a circle. What strange message was it trying to send us? I tried to discern a logic, a meaning, my childish brain running at full capacity. But the enigma remained. When I was old enough to talk (and unable to contain myself any longer), I asked my mother.

"Mama, what's that?"

"That? That's Themoon!" she replied, as if it were obvious.

Funny name for a pebble perched in the sky, I thought. I continued to observe it through the window, but with less concern now that I knew its name. It was the start of a great love story between Themoon and me. My pebble perched in the sky. In hindsight, I think that I have always remained that fascinated kid, arms outstretched on the grass, engulfed by emotions, tears streaming down my cheeks and splashing on the ground in bright little beads.

"Paul Vertune? Ah, yes, little Paul who is always daydreaming? He won't be much of a man, he's not suited for work!" people whispered among themselves.

When the villagers spoke about me, they pulled a doubtful face, which I hardly failed to notice. Despite my young age, I already discerned a negative connotation when people talked about daydreaming, as if dreaming were forbidden and emotion, criminal. After all, what harm was there in spending hours observing celestial bodies? I never felt as if I were committing a misdemeanor, let alone a felony. But a child's gaze obscures the grubby reality. Children cannot see their own hidden flaws, their own power struggles. I only understood the real issue at hand much later: idleness, that weakness of spirit that certain people sometimes master splendidly without anyone realizing. There in the countryside, idleness meant death, while life was wheat, that gold sprouting from the earth, the center of our lives. My village's economy depended on it. Wheat was a capricious crop that followed a strict life cycle in which the slightest mistake cost us dearly. Being born in the countryside left us very little choice in the end. It was wheat or exile, toil or starvation. Most of the village's inhabitants were attached to their roots and took over their ancestors' farms, working the land till they died. Their days consisted of nothing else. Wheat, always wheat, forevermore. I often accompanied the men to the fields and sat in a corner watching them. My brothers barely looked up, jealous of my still being allowed to enjoy such carefree days. As for my father, he cast a disdainful eye over me. His gaze, already heavy with reproach, seemed to hold me for an eternity.

Your turn will come, he seemed to be saying. *Just like everyone else here, you'll dig the earth, sow the seeds, lay out the plots, organize the harvests, scythe the stalks, pick up the wheat, negotiate the price with dishonest wholesalers, return home at night worn out, and go to bed with your back aching. And the next day, do the same thing, from dawn till dusk, every day that God grants you, without respite or rest. For the wheat won't wait. It never does. Then we'll see that exasperating smile wiped off your face.*

I was convinced my father hated me from the day I was born. He found me too different from him, more interested in thinking than doing. Out in the countryside, thinking was considered a virus to be eradicated. A destructive scourge, a disgrace, a family sacrilege. Don't think, just act—scythe the wheat, period. Thinking was a layabout's invention, a subterfuge to flee harsh reality, a cancer. My father didn't think. He worked hard, without ever taking refuge or shirking his male responsibilities. Quite my opposite. And I understood this as a child, thanks to that "cancer" dwelling within me. My mind frolicked ceaselessly, free as air, anxious to protect me from suffering. It constantly reinvented a reality in which I felt comfortable, like a bird in its nest lifting its beak to be fed. A quality my father abhorred above all else.

When I was five years old, destiny knocked at my door for the first time. My entire life since then has been built upon a succession of happenstances, strokes of fortune, coincidences—call them what you will. Me, I call them *signs of destiny.* Too bad if that expression seems naive. A path opened up to me that day and I threw myself onto it wholeheartedly, with neither remorse nor regret.

14

One Sunday, after mass, we all set off for the port of Arzon, which sits facing the vastness of the Atlantic Ocean on the western tip of the Rhuys Peninsula. Upon arrival, we spied a bunch of onlookers gathered by a ship, shouting with excitement and stroking the rusty hull of the massive vessel. Some, full of admiration, chatted with several bizarrely dressed men. I'd never seen such getups: flat hats with bobbles on top, blue-and-white-striped sweaters, navy-blue canvas pants, slim braided shoes. These characters looked as if they had stepped straight out of the future. My brothers ran over and stopped in front of them. No doubt accustomed to this, the men drily beheld the wide eyes staring at them with such admiration. My mother approached too, as did I, struck dumb by the mystery of these men in their strange uniforms. Where could they have come from? The moon, that pebble in the sky? Were they the ones responsible for its light? Was the ocean full of secret passages that took them all the way up there? My enthusiasm mounted as I drew nearer, excited at the idea of discovering the truth about my pebble. I gripped my mother's hand tightly, my heart pulsating in my chest like a soundly beaten drum. When we were beside them, I looked up, the better to take in their eccentric costumes. One of them knelt down, removed his strange hat, and placed it on my head.

"Now you're a sailor too!" the man exclaimed with a smile.

It's odd how this apparently trifling phrase resonated in my mind for years. Certain words mark us for the rest of our days. We retain the indelible trace of their letters like a tattoo. The fibers of the hat sitting on my head were deeply ingrained with the centuries of knowledge of what I assumed to be an ancient brotherhood. I felt all of its force, its energy, and its philosophy through that fabric. The man plucked his hat from me and placed it back on his head. Then he ruffled my hair, little suspecting that he had instilled in me an idea that would gnaw away at my mind for years to come, shaping the recesses of my brain like a sculptor working his stone, to lay the foundations of a vocation. The man then headed for the ship, climbed the steps to the gangway, and waved at the people massed below. Soon the sound of the engines began to thrum across the port. White foam surged from the stern, and exultant cries rose from the crowd of onlookers as the ship moved away from the quay. My gaze was fixed on my sailor as he stood waving his arms on deck, happy to be flying away to Themoon. The ship eventually disappeared from view amid the rolling reflections of the ocean, and the crowd slowly dispersed. As for me, I remained rooted to the spot, my eyes fixed seaward. Part of me had embarked with them that day, to confront the storms and the currents. I was now certain of my choice. One day I would be a sailor too. Like them. I would sail away on the big blue ocean, the sea breeze caressing my cheeks as I stood on deck, a goofy smile plastered across my lips. That is, if my father one day granted me this privilege.

4

The days passed peacefully in the Gulf of Morbihan. My father and brothers went off to the fields while I helped Mama in her daily chores. I gathered fruit from the garden, milked the cows, and fed the animals. Every morning we went to the village market to buy the various ingredients for dinner. The farmers' wives—forsaken by their husbands, whose mistresses, the crops, kept them busy—all rushed to the square to chat, to share their solitude. My mother's days were filled with drudgery, the same routine of endlessly repetitive, alienating chores. But Wednesday was laundry day, and thus different. I awaited it with impatience, counting off the days on an imaginary calendar, marking crosses on the invisible wall of time's passing. On Tuesday evenings, all the hair on my body would quiver with anticipation. I found it difficult to close my eyes, so hard was it to contain my excitement. I tossed and turned in bed, my heart pounding, my breathing rapid. The emotions were so intense that sometimes I trembled with fear at the thought of not being able to control them. They submerged me with all their might, all their volatility. Frightened by these convulsions, I turned my head to the window. Themoon hung resplendent in the sky, sometimes pale and puny, sometimes dazzlingly bright. Its golden rays spread like notes of silent music across the heavens, soothing my tormented mind.

As I lay on my straw pillow, my restless eyelids grew heavy under the lunar melody and I fell into a peaceful sleep.

In the morning we went to do our laundry at the washhouse, where my mother was a regular. The women of the village used to meet there at an allotted time in order to make this tiresome task jollier. I loved this moment above all else, that singular atmosphere full of gaiety, soap scenting the air, the uninhibited laughter of these women who, just for a few hours, were free of their husbands' authoritarian grips. The rest of the week they moved about their homes like ghosts. But in the intimacy of the dilapidated washhouse, they threw off the chains of the submissive wife and were reborn. They splashed about in a whirl of bubbles, smiling at life in a way they no longer smiled at their men. On Wednesdays I watched them play the roles of the women they'd been before marriage, and I marveled at the spectacle. Finally, they lay on the grass, breathless, with arms outstretched. I applauded their performance, a little sad that the play was at an end. Panting, my mother smiled broadly at me, full of a certain madness that had displaced reason, before slowly returning to her usual self.

It was over. We had to return to the farm. Darkness had fallen, and I gripped her hand tightly on the dirt track. She whispered tenderly in my ear to reassure me. The two of us were alone in the world, with the stars for lanterns. She let go of my hand when we arrived home and paid me scant attention until the following day. No doubt she feared my father would reproach her for showing me excessive emotion. In spite of my young age, I understood that relations between the two sexes were very complex, separated by a river of emotion that would sometimes spill over or dry up. Children are marked for life by the upbringing they receive. That is how I grew up, amid a whirlpool of emotions nipped in the bud, suppressed, without realizing that one day all the corpses at the bottom of the river would float to the surface.

◆　◆　◆

18

One July afternoon, not long after my sixth birthday, my brother Jacques taught me to dig for clams. I hung on his every word, listening attentively to his wise instruction. He showed me how to find the best spots, scratch in the sand, and not strain my back too much. I threw myself enthusiastically into the hunt for my first shellfish, ready to do anything to amaze my parents and shine in the eyes of my father. A few hours later, my bucket remained as empty as a cloudless sky. Jacques's, however, was full to the brim. Of all my siblings, he was my father's favorite, the eldest, the most productive, the one who gathered the most wheat and collected the most shellfish for Sunday lunch. The family couldn't praise him enough, all agreeing he would be the next owner of the Vertune farm. My exact opposite. Over time, an affective hierarchy developed in the family. Our brotherly rivalry grew more palpable each day, although I managed to avoid being seen as a threat, thanks to the paradoxical advantage of always falling short. Jacques was fond of his little brother. He saw me as a playmate rather than an adversary. And it was this perception that convinced him to take me under his wing. Might as well make allies where one can.

So on that afternoon, the last rays of sun glimmered over the darkness of the ocean and I resigned myself to returning home empty-handed. I pedaled toward the farm. A few yards from the house, I heard raised voices. I laid my bicycle down in the grass and silently skirted the animal pen. The imprisoned beasts covered the sound of my steps with their scornful lowing at the human race. I slid along the wall until I caught a glimpse of my parents locked in discussion.

"What are we going to do with him?" bellowed my father with such disdain that I immediately knew he was referring to me.

"Give him a chance, take him to the fields, show him how to work the land."

"He's useless, that kid, there's nothing to be done about him. He's not like his brothers, he's got no backbone, no courage, he's like a little girl!"

"You're too hard on him," protested my mother. "He's different from the others, it's true, but that's no reason to scorn him."

"We'll see about that. Tomorrow I'll take him to the fields with us."

My fate was playing out before my eyes. The die was cast, the deck stacked. I felt the injustice of being just a child, not allowed to have my say. My father looked in my direction. I started and hid behind the wall, curled into a ball, my stomach knotted with fear. I was scared he'd come for me in my hiding place, furious at being spied on by his own son. But he went back inside and I heard nothing more. Night had now fallen. In a corner of the sky, Themoon still smiled upon me, its vast craters like dimples. Crouching behind the wall, like a prisoner on the run, I sensed that my carefree days were coming to an end. The afternoons at the washhouse, reveling in the beauty of those liberated women, would soon be no more than a distant memory. Clouds began to fill the sky, dark and sinister, like the years ahead. It was time to become a man.

5

My father woke me before dawn. His face loomed over me in the dark, his hair still tousled with sleep. He put his finger to his lips and beckoned me to follow him. All my brothers were still fast asleep. The house was completely silent. I rubbed my eyes, sat up slowly on the hay mattress, and fumbled in the half-light. As I walked across the room, I felt a strange mix of curiosity and fear. Why had he woken me so early and left my brothers to sleep? Outside, the cool air caressed my face and I felt the moist morning dew on my bare feet. My father sadly watched me from beside the animal pen. I sat down on a piece of wood. He furrowed his brow, preparing his solemn speech.

"Today I'm going to teach you to till the land," he said coldly.

"Yes, Papa."

"Then, in September, I will introduce you to the village schoolmaster. You'll go to class in the morning and work the fields in the afternoon."

He paused for a few seconds, his eyes boring into mine.

"I want you to become a man, Paul, who gets up early and works all day long without grumbling, or dreaming, or thinking—who simply works his plot and feeds his wife and children by the sweat of his brow. If you're not up to it, there's nothing I can do for you. Out here in the countryside, you're born in the field and you die in the field. Those who don't like it leave. Got it?"

"Yes, Papa."

"Go wake your brothers while I get the tools ready. Tell them we'll be leaving in fifteen minutes."

I ran to the bedroom and roused my brothers. They understood that my turn had come. Childhood was drawing to an end. My first adult responsibilities had appeared. We breakfasted in silence and set off without a word, tools in hand. My father led the way, proud as a rooster, greeting the people we passed as we went. He couldn't wait to see the sweat run down my brow and hear me beg him for a break, exhausted by the heat. When we reached the field, everyone went straight to their posts, heads bowed, like good little soldiers. I found myself at the edge of the field not knowing where to start, having never received any training in how to work the land.

"Paul, come here," yelled my father.

"Yes, Papa," I replied, dashing toward him.

"For the first few months you'll watch how we work and give us a hand whenever we tell you to."

"Yes, Papa."

I did as I was told, frustrated at no longer being able to enjoy my mother's tenderness and her warm smiles. As in any organization, farming obeys a hierarchy established by time and experience. Nobody was exempt from the rules. Everyone started at the bottom of the ladder and worked their way up on merit, according to the amounts of wheat sown or harvested. My first task—lending a hand to whoever required it most—was the initial rung in that long ascent to responsibility. For the first time in my life I had a *job*. That word held a place of considerable importance in my father's mind, being part and parcel of the human condition. To my mind, however, it did not bode well at all.

I swallowed my pride and threw myself into the work, eager to shine in my father's eyes and redeem myself. I attended to everyone's needs according to their progress, coordinating the distribution of tools in such a way that there was no dead time. I brought water when their mouths were dry, handed out the midday meals, and packed away the equipment come evening. Out in the fields, my eternal optimism always prevailed. I ended up enjoying this job of handyman; it suited my active mind, my need to always be moving around. And helping others suited my sensitive personality. An unshakable smile lit up my face, in spite of the exhausting days, the sunburn, and the blisters on my hands. To keep my spirits high, I sang my mother's hymns. My brothers, recognizing the melody of their curtailed childhood, hummed along when my father was otherwise occupied. They were all wary of my father, except for Jacques, who had a special relationship with him. From time to time, my father raised his head above the golden stalks swaying in the wind, scanning the field to glimpse my face, convinced he had an idiot son, a good-for-nothing. When he finally caught sight of me, he'd yell, just for the pleasure of trying to break my optimistic spirit. He didn't understand why I was still smiling. He had hardly smiled for years. Decades. Millennia. Once he'd vented his spleen, he returned to work, mumbling inanities into his beard, like the elderly ruminating upon their expended lives. Jacques, stupefied by the unshifting smile that illuminated my face, quickly grew jealous. He set out to destroy my optimism by reproaching me for not carrying out my tasks quickly enough, claiming I was handicapping his progress. I stupidly apologized, so as not to stir his hate any further, and redoubled my efforts, indefatigable, until he could no longer reproach me for anything. Then he would stop his little ploy, tired of yelling and gesticulating for naught, having understood that nothing and nobody could stymie my desire to prove myself, particularly in my father's eyes.

By the end of the summer, my hands were cracked with scars, slashed by the ungrateful wheat, and my back was bent by the weight of the tools. Mama had to step in so I could rest. I was consumed with the urge to show my worth. My father, who had succeeded in bringing me to my knees, affirmed what he had foreseen.

"You're nothing but a shameful little girl; you'll never become a man," he told me one morning while my mother's back was turned.

Then he headed off to the fields, accompanied by my brothers and their tools. When they had disappeared down the track, I sadly lowered my head. The whole world was collapsing beneath my feet. I was seized by a feeling of failure. Never would I shine as brightly in my father's eyes as Themoon did in the sky. Truth has an acid taste. My father would never love me. Summer was coming to an end. My mother couldn't help me anymore and I had to go back to the fields. Work became routine, alienating. My former drive had left me, replaced by indifference. Out in the fields I thought about the sailors in their beautiful striped outfits, their hair ruffled by the ocean breeze. I would have loved to join them, greet the crowd in the port, chat with curious onlookers, and sail off far away to live my dream. But I had to face the facts. I was just a farmer's boy, filthy with the soil of his field, whose only fate was to till the earth until he died. The rest was just an illusion, the bittersweet fruit of my imagination. I hopped with impatience, waiting for day's end, brooding on my discontent in a kind of mental confusion, and dreaming of elsewhere. I wasn't like the others. And I already knew that this difference would be a problem. The Vertune family would never accept one of its members wanting to make his own way in the world.

6

One September morning my father walked me briskly down the dirt road to the village. I remained silent beside him. We stopped in front of a stonework building. Inside, a small bearded man was pacing back and forth. When he saw us, he came out and extended his hand. My father shook it mechanically, with no warmth, and left as silently as he had arrived. I looked up at the strange man, who was scrutinizing me from behind his round spectacles. His thick beard contrasted with his fine features. He exuded a pleasantness that immediately inspired my trust.

"Hello, Paul," he said in a soft voice. "My name is Monsieur Duquerre. I'm the village schoolmaster."

"Good day to you, sir," I replied shyly.

"Do you know what a schoolmaster is?"

"Yes. It's the man who teaches the classes!" I answered proudly.

"Exactly! Welcome to Brillac School. Follow me, I'll show you around the place."

I took the schoolmaster's hand. He was clearly surprised to feel my little hand in his and stared at me, dumbfounded. I sensed that he was touched by such a gesture. He stopped in the shadow of the building and gave me a lukewarm smile. Then we entered, passed several empty rooms, and came to an empty courtyard. The schoolmaster explained that this was where the children played when they weren't studying. My brothers sometimes mentioned their mornings at school, but they had never said anything about playing. They all spoke of this establishment with the same disdain, particularly Jacques, who was bored to death here. But I thought this schoolyard was beautiful. It was huge and dotted with plane trees conducive to children's games. Everything else about the place was fantastic too, so different from the settings I was used to. I couldn't wait to enjoy this magical environment with my schoolmates.

I could tell that the schoolmaster noticed my wonderment, but he didn't remark upon it. He led me into a room with a commanding view of the whole playground and invited me to sit down. Handing me a glass of water, he said, "So, Paul, did you enjoy this visit?"

"Yes," I replied, awestruck.

"From now on you will spend your mornings here. You will join my class, starting tomorrow, and you will take lessons up until the School Certificate."

"What's the School Certificate?"

"It's a diploma you will receive at the end of your studies. With that you will be able to do whatever you wish in life. Do you know what you want to do later on?"

"I would like to be a sailor, sir."

"That's a fine profession," he said, a little awkward at this avowal. "But you will have to learn to read and write, for you can't become a sailor if you're illiterate."

"What's illiterate?"

"It's when a person can't read or write."

"Like Papa and Mama?"

Monsieur Duquerre didn't answer. He simply took me by the hand and led me back outside to where my father was waiting. My father didn't look up as he shook the schoolmaster's hand again. He was usually so sure of himself, but now I saw shame in his eyes, as if he felt inferior to Monsieur Duquerre. The schoolmaster went back inside.

On the way home, I didn't dare ask my father if he was illiterate, for fear of angering him. I simply observed his gait, that of a farmer worn down by work. That evening, when the farm fell silent and my brothers slept, I thought about the schoolmaster, his bushy beard and his round spectacles; the playground with its plane trees, their trunks devoid of branches; the sandpit in which everything was imaginable; the classrooms that would soon be filled. I imagined myself in the middle of all these children in a hurry to be taught so they might stand on their own two feet, far from the wheat fields. The schoolmaster's words resonated in my head: *You will have to learn to read and write, for you can't become a sailor if you're illiterate.* Would I be able to learn those skills?

My next few years were accompanied by the sound of the schoolmaster's whistle and the swoosh of the scythe. I quickly learned to read and write, fascinated by the world of literature and knowledge. I was the first to arrive for Monsieur Duquerre's lesson every morning, and I sat at my desk impatient to wrestle with the new knowledge—which was never enough to satisfy my curiosity. The schoolmaster was initially surprised at such diligence but eventually got used to my enthusiasm. He too began to arrive earlier and earlier. What more beautiful gift could he receive from a pupil than that they eat up his every word? I devoured his teaching without dropping a single crumb. He quite naturally developed a fondness for me—perhaps even love, I don't know. The word in the village was that, despite his erudition, he lived alone, surrounded by his books. Knowledge frightened country folk, as did those who promoted it. In those days, nothing was more important than feeding one's family. Most people had never ventured more than six miles from the village. What point was there in being educated?

Besides reading, writing, and arithmetic, I studied geography, the history of France, and ethics. One winter evening, Monsieur Duquerre

27

taught me to recognize the constellations in the sky. He pointed out that Themoon was written as two words, *the moon*—another sign that my childhood was fast receding. He smiled as I blushed with shame at having shown my ignorance. Later, I was astonished when he pointed out our geographical location on a map of the world. My naive eyes couldn't get over seeing the oceans, the continents, and the poles clearly marked on the laminated card. The blue expanses on the map made me think of the sailors. I imagined myself in the future, wearing my uniform and navigating the currents of the Gulf Stream, glimpsing the tip of Cape Horn, and braving the devastating gales of the Roaring Forties. That made me happy. I memorized the names of the countries, their capitals and major cities, as well as the French departments, prefectures, and subprefectures. I would recite them during afternoons in the fields. My father watched me without uttering a word, with that barely veiled jealousy that the uneducated often bear toward the learned. Knowledge was within reach, I just had to pluck it from my schoolmaster's teachings. Inside the school walls I recovered a taste for life, and despite the afternoons of drudgery, I felt as if I could reach out and touch some of my wildest dreams. School was a gateway to a bright future in which everything seemed possible.

The year 1939 marked a turning point in history. Evil gnawed at the edges of Europe. Hitler invaded Poland, causing France and Britain to declare war on Nazi Germany. The chaos extended as far as the frontiers of the Soviet Union. Europe became a giant inferno in which humanity slowly perished. Our country was now at war. The world map hanging on the wall was out of date. German domination now stretched far beyond its borders. Shortly after the announcement of France entering the war, Monsieur Duquerre drew me aside and explained the conflict raging nearby. Tears began to run down his cheeks as his detailed lesson drew to a close.

"Why are you crying, sir?" I asked, moved.

"War is an awful thing that takes everything we have," he declared as he wept.

"Did war take something from you, sir?"

"Yes, my father."

"How?"

"Dead in the trenches of Verdun during the Great War. A shell fell on him. He went there to protect his homeland. Nobody protected him." He wiped his tears away with the back of his hand. "I'm going to show you something."

Taking an envelope from his satchel, he ran his fingers gently down the edge and withdrew a small folded sheet of paper, which he handed to me.

"You can read it if you like," he said, as if offering me a piece of treasure.

I carefully unfolded the sheet of paper. It was a letter, in delicate handwriting. What I read touched me deeply.

Dear Édouard,

I write you this letter to tell you that everything is fine here. We rise at dawn each day and contemplate the German line facing us. The Germans, who are really not so different from us, also watch that we do not advance into enemy territory. We wait in our hidey-holes, a bit like how you do at school when you play with the other pupils. You see, when all is said and done, as much as we may have grown up, we are nevertheless all just big children.

Last week, for Christmas, we left our trenches for the first time and chatted with the enemy, exchanged gifts, and played football together. I must admit I no longer understand the point of this war. Yet we are still here, waiting in the winter chill.

Édouard, my darling son, I want you to know that I love you with all my heart, that I think about you and your mother day and night, that you are with me wherever I go, and that I will love you both always. If something were to happen to me here, I want you to be strong, my son, to become a man despite your tender age, and look after your mother. You are my two angels and I will never desert you, wherever I may be. I hope to come home soon and hold you in my arms. I love you both.

Papa

I reread the letter in order to better grasp the meaning of the words, imagining my schoolmaster's father in his dirty hidey-hole, then kicking a ball around with the enemy. *What a curious contrast,* I thought. The First World War had caused millions of deaths, scarring whole families for life, cutting down so many innocents. Amid this incoherent farce, some soldiers had made peace for the space of a quick match before holing back up in their dens again. I couldn't help thinking about my father. Under a deluge of shells, would he have understood that life is too short to carry one's most intimate feelings to the grave? Would he too have set down on a blank sheet of paper the words I'd been waiting for since my birth? Monsieur Duquerre slid the letter back into the envelope as he wiped away the last of his tears. He told me he must go to Rennes, the capital of Brittany, to look after his mother and meet with the school's inspector, a man who had high ambitions for him.

I returned to my parents' farm with a heavy heart. When my father saw me arrive, he told me I was just a good-for-nothing who would never be a man. I went to lie down in the garden and dozed in the shade of the apple trees. I felt comfortable under their tranquil branches, alone in the world.

◆　◆　◆

The following Monday, Monsieur Duquerre told me he was leaving for Rennes. His mother was very sick and was counting on him to take care of her, as his father had instructed in his letter. He promised to get me a scholarship to study in Rennes. He would be replaced by another schoolmaster. The inspector came to fetch him in a black car. Monsieur Duquerre shook my hand coldly so as not to arouse any suspicions regarding our secret relationship, then got in the car, which drove off down the road. I never saw him again, despite his promises and efforts on my behalf. He left me to my fate, alone in my childhood village.

I was angry with him for a long time, until one day in a library, many years later, I saw his name on a list of those who had died for France. He had been conscripted to defend the motherland, like his father before him, and had been shot in an ambush close to the German border, in a little village near Alsace. Had he thought of me the day he fell, his chest riddled with bullets? He, the little schoolmaster whose existence had been ravaged by war, who had devoted his entire life to helping others, was now dead, lying in the cold ground.

I returned to school the day after his departure, but my heart wasn't in it. The new schoolmaster was too busy writing books and had no time to spare me outside of school hours. His only effort was to lend me a few books, which I devoured and gave back to him. A vast emotional emptiness seized me. Monsieur Duquerre had been much more than a schoolmaster. Over time he had become a real father to me. Now I would have to do without.

Something had changed in the village. We soon witnessed the arrival of a battalion of Nazis with orders to secure the Brittany beaches in case the enemy tried to land there. They came to the farm to seize our wheat. My father objected vociferously and was roughed up in front of his family. The German soldiers roared with laughter as he lay on the ground, his face covered in blood. I pitied him and helped him back up, but he didn't thank me for it. The Nazis left, their packs stuffed with grain. We were now the children of an occupied France, a republic split in two. The red and white colors of fascism were everywhere, stamped with the hard, crooked lines of the black swastika. We learned to live in terror of the enemy, who would frequently stop us to check our papers. It seemed like they were searching for something specific as they scrutinized us and scanned our ID cards from every angle, looking for the slightest indication of forgery. Later we learned the horrific truth: they were seeking Jews to murder in their camps in Poland. Many men from my village were taken for Compulsory Work Service. My father was lucky to escape this when they came for him. The large truck pulled into the yard, packed tightly full of men, and there was no room for him. Was it destiny or purely chance? I couldn't say. Life's long journey contains plenty of mysteries, the origins of which we shall never know.

My father continued tending his fields, as if the enemy patrolling the edges of his land every day were invisible to him. The wheat was clearly more important than anything else. He seemed rooted in his field for eternity, like the ears of wheat he'd been scything since the dawn of his existence. Yet one October afternoon he died.

We never knew the precise circumstances of his death. What had he been thinking before he passed away? Had he repented for his behavior? For a long time I imagined his death as I went to sleep at night, alone in my bed. A romantic end, as in the books I devoured. Standing amid the plants, which never disputed his authority, my father reveled in the whisper of the wind through the golden stalks, moved by their oceanic stirring as he contemplated the mysterious shadow sweeping across his field. Submerged in a cocktail of emotions, worn out from a lifetime of drudgery, he crumbled to the ground, his eyes raised heavenward to the moon's diurnal smile. By a strange twist of fate, the Reaper cut him down with the same dexterity my father displayed when scything the ears of wheat. Just goes to show there's no such thing as coincidence in life.

7

It was a gray and rainy day. Brittany was wearing its autumnal cloak, the trees their ochre robes. When we saw him lying lifeless in a wooden box, we had to accept the reality. He was quite dead. I drew near the coffin and perused his face. I thought I could discern a slight smile. In death, my father displayed a semblance of grace. He lay there, cold as ice, hard as stone, but his face was serene. Perhaps he had to die in order to reveal his true nature to us. I felt nothing that day as I stood before his final resting place—neither sorrow nor rage, nor anything at all. I gazed at him with the same indifference he had shown me the day of my birth. I wondered only what would happen to my brothers and me without him. We stood as if frozen before this lifeless, soulless body. I was surprised to see Jacques, whom my father loved most, hold back his tears. He stared at the whiteness of the body with a teenager's fascination at the stillness of death. My mother bent to kiss her husband's forehead. As her lips brushed the icy skin, she pulled back, as if surprised by the chill of the corpse.

We buried my father the next day. All the villagers gathered to pay their respects and lay flowers on his coffin. They acknowledged his courage and lamented this man departed too soon. They consoled my mother, now a widow, standing rigid in front of her husband's coffin. Then we laid him in the earth. As the coffin descended into the dark hole of the freshly dug grave, everybody wept. Such hypocrisy. No one liked my father. *Why are they weeping for a man who never shed a tear for anyone?* The ceremony drew to a close and the villagers dried their crocodile tears. We headed back to the farm. The joy of baptism is counterpointed by the despair of death. There's no consistency in this grotesque masquerade.

On the way we passed a few German soldiers; they were too involved with warmongering to console us. They nevertheless had enough respect not to bother the funeral party, all dressed in black. Death frightens even the fiercest soldiers.

When we reached the farm, a meeting was held, stretching late into the night. Decisions were made. My father's farm and fields now belonged to my mother, in accordance with their premarital agreement. The Vertune sons would work the land together, and when Jacques was ready he would take over running the family concern. Our uncles would take turns helping us for the first few years, after which Jacques would assume complete responsibility for the farm and for selling the wheat. The young man was considered the most capable of feeding the Vertune family. When they told us of their plans, I shuddered, imagining spending the rest of my days enslaved to those fields I hated everything about, even the smell of the earth defiled by my father's body. I felt caught in a trap, a hostage to fate without any consideration of the individual and his views. It was a trap with no escape, no exit. I would be chained to the land, like generations of men before me. The question of my studies now seemed anathema, my family's survival believed to be more important than the idle pursuit of knowledge. My adolescence began the day my father died.

The next day, I rose at dawn to go to the fields, far from the books that had so recently been my joy. I watched my childhood dream float away on the golden seas of the wheat fields, the stalks undulating in the wind like waves. My brother Jacques, now promoted to master and commander, turned into an even crueler tyrant than my father, less assiduous in his work but better equipped to do as little as possible himself. Jacques had understood when very young that you don't command by breaking your back but by getting the psychological upper hand over everyone else. Some men are as changeable as the wind, shifting direction like a weathervane to pursue their own interests. Jacques was one such man. From then on, he had no allies in the fields. The solidarity of our childhood dissipated like a veil of mist over the sea, and we were all subject to his iron yoke.

I learned to become a man during those years, to grit my teeth, to imagine life more than live it. On our way to the fields each morning, we passed the school. I looked at the facade of the building in which Monsieur Duquerre, with his round spectacles, had taught me so much. Sometimes nostalgia overwhelmed me. But I didn't lose hope. Soon the hour would come when I'd be free for good. In the meantime, I might as well keep smiling. My intuition would take care of the rest. Optimism always triumphs in the end, despite the assertions of those, like my father, who never smile.

8

The date was April 17, 1943, and the war raged above our heads, as British bombers dropped their payloads on the Rhuys Peninsula with the aim of annihilating the German forces based there. The screams of the villagers as the bombs fell suggested the coming of the apocalypse.

"Quick, to the cellar!" yelled my mother, terrified at the idea of losing one of her sons.

We scurried down the stairs and gathered in the farmhouse cellar. Outside, it was pure panic as people rushed for shelter yet again. Nobody had asked for war, yet here it was, ravaging our crops and houses without our say-so. There were only two solutions amid this chaos: escape or endure. The world is often binary. An exodus to the unoccupied zone, a couple of hundred miles away, was possible, thanks to the support of Resistance networks, but it would mean leaving behind family, friends, house, and land. Unfortunately for me—dreaming of pastures new—nobody in our circle seemed eager to leave the area. Nobody wanted to abandon land inherited from their ancestors, despite the bombs raining down on their farms, their cattle, and their livelihoods. So we had to endure. And enduring meant withstanding the injustices of the German soldiers, their incessant ID checks, sometimes even their violence. Whenever we were stopped by them, they would rant at us in their incomprehensible and strange-sounding language.

So that morning we sheltered in the cellar where the cider was usually stored, waiting for the deluge of bombs to end. Mama huddled on the floor praying, hands clasped in front of her chest, tightly clutching her crucifix and murmuring inaudible hymns, imploring the Lord's protection. I watched my mother silently, unnoticed. She was still beautiful, despite the lines that grief had etched into her face. I adored everything about her: her large almond eyes, her slightly upturned nose, the ponytail into which she always gathered her hair. Crouching, surrounded by her children, she prayed for the end of this murderous madness that sometimes possesses men when they no longer listen to their hearts. The room smelled strongly of cider. Outside, the animals bellowed and howled, terrified by the bombs. *Man is crazy,* they must have thought. Jacques sat there impassive, simply waiting for us to be able to return to the fields. He resembled my father. Both of them shared the same capacity for nonreflection, for remaining unencumbered by emotions. I was the exact opposite. As for Pierre and Guy, they hugged each other, trembling with fear. They also shared a resemblance, a subtle mixture of my father and mother, the happy medium, but I was never particularly close to either of them. I simply prayed that the bombs wouldn't hit us. We heard the long whistle of their fall, initially distant and then closer and closer, before they hit the ground with a deafening crash that shook the earth. With each bomb, I gritted my teeth hard, thinking of the victims, the unlucky ones. Sometimes you are just in the wrong place at the wrong time. Once, the bombs fell a few dozen yards from the house, the closest ripping through the raspberry bushes of my childhood, and I thought my last hour had come. War scars those who have known it up close, haunting them for eternity. In later years, a slamming door or exploding fireworks would cause me to tense up and recall those moments spent crouching in the farmhouse cellar, waiting for death.

The planes disappeared from the Brittany sky. We ventured out of our lair like hunted foxes to find that not a single bomb had touched any part of the farm. Fate had been kind to us this time. My mother picked up her household chores where she'd left off, without saying a word, solid as a rock. My brother ordered us back to the fields; we were late with the sowing and had another week's work ahead of us. To my dismay, Jacques had refused any help from our uncles, preferring to toil from dawn till dusk. He wanted to prove his tenacity to the family as a point of honor, or rather ego. We set off for the fields, which I hated with every fiber of my being.

Halfway there, a group of soldiers demanded to see our papers. We each showed them in turn. One of them yelled a few words in German—I really didn't like that language at all. Then they pushed us to the ground and began kicking the hell out of us. An officer's boot pounded into my ribs, arms, and legs, and I screamed with pain each time the rough leather met my skin. They howled with laughter at our terror. When they tired of their violent game, they threw us in a truck. Jacques resisted, pushing one of them away. Their chief lifted his rifle and brought the butt crashing down into Jacques's face, smashing his nose in a spurt of blood. Jacques stared at his aggressor, stunned. He seemed surprised at such cruelty, which was ironic given how tyrannical his behavior had been since my father died. But we all meet our match at some point. Jacques understood this and lowered his head, clutching his nose.

The truck drove off. We looked at one another, not understanding what was happening. The Germans talked among themselves in their barbaric language, paying us no mind. We hugged each other, the tension and anxiety palpable. Jacques held his nose, head bowed, cursing the Germans with all his being. Blood dripped from his nose, pooling at his feet. Guy and Pierre stared at me strangely, with a mixture of complicity, incomprehension, and a certain warmth, that brotherly affection my father had patiently strived to blunt. Sibling unity was restored a little in the cramped space of the vehicle. I felt at ease among them, despite our uncomfortable situation.

The truck pulled up in front of a huge white stone farmhouse. We got out, fearing what the soldiers had in store for us. A German beckoned us over to a barn a short distance away in which hundreds of hay bales were stored. He pointed at another, larger truck parked nearby and mimed loading the bales onto the vehicle. I breathed a sigh of relief. It was to be forced labor, not death. Another soldier went inside the farmhouse and emerged with a short man whom he pushed into the barn, sending him flying to the floor. The man looked up at us, his eyes full of rage. He nodded at us in greeting. It was Monsieur Blanchart, the village mayor. It took us three hours to load the hay bales onto the truck. When we were done, the Krauts drove off without even a word of thanks, leaving us all standing there.

"Filthy Germans," exclaimed Monsieur Blanchart angrily. "They took all my wheat and all my cattle, and now they've commandeered my barn."

"What exactly do they want it for?" asked Jacques.

"A munitions store."

"And your hay?" I asked.

"They'll burn it, of course! What do you think they'll do with it?" he replied. "But we can't do anything, nobody can. This damn war will never end."

"They say the Americans will come," said Jacques.

"The Americans have got other fish to fry, believe you me!" replied Monsieur Blanchart. "Anyway, come along to the house for something to drink. A little human warmth won't hurt in these sad times."

The farmhouse was full of the pleasant scent of freshly baked bread. He invited us to sit.

"Mathilde, bring us some glasses of water!" he shouted in the direction of the kitchen.

"Yes, Papa, I'm coming," said a younger voice.

"How are things at the farm?" he asked my eldest brother.

"Good. We're a bit behind with the plowing, but nothing serious," replied Jacques, then he scowled. "If the Krauts hadn't grabbed us this morning, we'd have made some progress."

"Don't talk to me about those parasites," said Monsieur Blanchart with annoyance. "I won't sleep soundly till they've gone!"

"Me neither," agreed Jacques.

The sound of clinking glasses came from the kitchen. Light steps approached, steps that barely touched the floor, and a girl appeared, carrying a tray with our drinks. This was the first time I set eyes on Mathilde Blanchart. My heart began to race, my palms grew moist, and I felt the blood drain from my face. She walked forward silently, concentrating so as not to spill the water, her long hair flowing over her shoulders. Her fair skin contrasted starkly with our own sun-weathered complexions. She must have spent most of her time shut up in the house. Women didn't have much of a choice in those days. They were born, grew up helping their mothers, got married, had children, took care of the household tasks, then died, worn out by domestic chores. No emancipation or liberty; men determined everything. Only a few, more resilient women managed to succeed in this battle between the sexes.

Mathilde Blanchart placed the tray on the table and served us our refreshments. I watched her, seduced by the calm dexterity of her hands. When she was done, her father motioned for her to leave us, and she disappeared into the kitchen. *Does Monsieur Blanchart hide his daughter to keep her from covetous eyes, protecting his treasure so no one can get close?* In a village of 150 souls, everyone knew each other. Rumors circulated as fast as the wind, rushing from house to house with the comings and goings of the inhabitants. We knew that the village mayor had a daughter, but nobody had ever seen her.

We drank our water, thanked the mayor for his warm hospitality, and headed back to our fields, hoping we wouldn't be pressed into service again by a German patrol. I thought of Mathilde as we walked, her white skin and her long flowing locks. She had paid me no attention, not even a glance, an indifference that made me a little annoyed. I felt the first stirrings of male ego, the same ego that was ravaging our countryside and our animals, and would be the source of much misfortune to come. I was already feeling the full force of love's first torments. At fourteen years old, my knowledge of the subject was minimal—nonexistent, in fact. The only love I had ever known was between my mother and me. But these stirrings of emotion for Mathilde were quite different, more visceral. This love took root almost imperceptibly before gradually extending its long tentacles, like an octopus gripping a fisherman's arm. The image of Mathilde soon came to haunt me day and night. Her face hung before me as I scythed the wheat. I smelled her imaginary scent as I drifted off to sleep, and I dreamed that, in the seclusion of her father's barn, her extended hands invited me to enter her kingdom, the hay bales crackling with the sparks of my passion. I awoke to the silence of the night, covered in sweat. My beloved moon smiled down through the window while my brothers snored around me. At mealtimes I simply gazed at my plate, letting Jacques scarf my uneaten rations. My stomach was too preoccupied with fighting against the frustration of not being able to approach Mathilde. I soon had to face the facts: I was in love with the young woman and sick with the lack of reciprocity.

9

One Sunday morning, when I could take it no more, I pretended to have an awful stomachache. I lay in bed writhing in simulated pain. Mama wanted to call the doctor, but I begged her not to. She relented, kissed my forehead, and set off to church with my brothers. I got up and dressed, happy to have completed the first step in my plan. For a while now I had been observing Monsieur Blanchart at church, how he always attended on his own, leaving Mathilde shut up at the farm. I knew that his wife had died a few years earlier, but why hide his daughter away?

Time was of the essence. I grabbed my eldest brother's bicycle and pedaled at breakneck speed in the direction of the Blanchart farm. As I approached, I was surprised to see several German trucks parked alongside the barn. Caught up in my passion, I had entirely forgotten their requisitioning of the building. I hid behind a bush and cursed this flaw in my plan. Those lousy Germans were everywhere. Not satisfied with preventing us from living our normal lives, they now deprived me of the possibility of making my romantic dreams a reality. *I just wish this stupid war would end,* I thought. But, Germans or no, my desires demanded action. I was ready to risk my life to get close to Mathilde. So I discreetly raised my head above the bush and strategically appraised the situation. The Blanchart farmhouse, located a hundred yards from the barn, appeared quiet. There was no sign of soldiers patrolling the area, just two sentries standing guard outside the barn. Rifles on shoulders, they stared into the distance. It was not going to be easy. The farmhouse was surrounded by thick forest, which would provide me with cover to advance. But the trees ended thirty yards from the house. My only option then would be to run across the open ground as fast as I could, a perilous tactic given the German fears about the Resistance. They would shoot me on sight.

Seeds of fear began to sprout in the well-plowed furrows of my resolve. *This is utter madness,* I thought. *I don't even know if Mathilde is there.* What was the point of dodging German bullets, of risking my life, if I didn't even get to speak to her? Maybe I really was crazy, unable to control this fanciful desire instead of waiting for the war to end to declare my love. But before giving up, I cast one final, sad gaze in the direction of the farmhouse. One detail caught my attention. A window that had been closed when I arrived was now open. It was on the other side of the building from the Germans, hidden from their view. Destiny had served up proof of Mathilde's presence on a silver platter.

A wave of elation washed over me. I headed into the forest abutting the Blanchart property. Thorns scratched at my skin, and I grabbed a piece of wood to beat a path through the vegetation. I made swift progress. There are magic moments in life where the world around us ceases to exist and all that matters is our pleasure in succumbing to an urge. Lowering my guard that day was the first major error of my life. A hand roughly seized my shoulder, violently pulling me to the ground. I found myself looking up into the furious face of a German soldier aiming his rifle at me. I closed my eyes and thought of my mother's face. *"Achtung! Kapitän!"* yelled the German, his lips flecked with saliva like a dog that has seized a hunted bird. A stream of urine coursed down my thigh, soaking my pants. My father had been right: I was nothing but a little girl. Papa's scornful face floated before my mind's eye. The German was screaming incomprehensible words. I would soon be joining the father I hated so much. My story was coming to an end. A German bullet would punch through my skin, rip my flesh apart, and send my guts spilling across the forest floor. I regretted lying to my mother. She would see my empty bed and worry about my absence while my soul glided over the fields toward the firmament. From up there I would watch her tears of concern, full of guilt at not having been able to control my passions. My mother would never get over it. I was just a good-for-nothing, an imbecile. They'd been right all along.

The expected gunshot never came. I heard the distant shouts of another soldier and the cracking of branches underfoot as he ran toward us.

"*Halt! Das ist ein Kind,*"[1] he shouted breathlessly.

The soldier with the gun trained on me stopped yelling and snapped to attention. The approaching steps grew louder and I felt the rasping breath of the man who had been running toward us.

"Who are you?" he asked in French with a strong German accent.

"I . . . I . . ." My eyes were still shut tight.

"Open your eyes!" he ordered.

I slowly opened my eyes and found myself face to face with a soldier whose uniform was different from the others, darker. The man looked to be in his forties, with short, very blond hair, almost Scandinavian in appearance. His eyes were as blue as the sea. *He's handsome,* I thought. He gave some orders to the other soldier, who briskly nodded and moved off into the woods. The man turned back to me and looked me up and down, noticing the patch of urine between my legs. I blushed.

"Are you in the Resistance?" he asked.

"No," I stuttered, coming to my senses.

"What are you up to, then?"

"Nothing, sir."

---

1   Translation: "Stop! It's just a child."

"Why are you here, then? Tell me!" he screamed, pointing the dark barrel of his pistol at me. Shaking, I decided to tell him the truth.

"I . . . wanted . . . to . . . go to the Blanchart farm," I said with difficulty, pointing toward the farmhouse.

"Why?"

"To . . . see . . . Mathilde . . ."

"Who is Mathilde?"

"Monsieur Blanchart's . . . daughter."

"Why do you want to see her?" he asked skeptically.

"Because . . ."

"Why? Answer me!" he screamed again.

"Because I love her," I replied, immediately regretting my response.

He froze, seeming incapacitated by such a declaration. What place had love amid all this unspeakable barbarity? The man had probably forgotten the very definition of the word, repressed deep inside of his being and double-locked in a safe.

"You love her?" he asked, eyes wide.

"Yes . . ."

The pistol barrel suddenly withdrew. I breathed freely again. His eyes bored deep into mine. There was something different about this man, something human. He was clearly wondering about the veracity of my claim as he scanned my face for the slightest trace of a lie. He paced around me, stroking his stubbly beard, before glancing over at his subordinate, who seemed more interested in the beauty of the trees than any possible threats. Having apparently settled the matter in his mind, he crouched beside me.

"Is it true, what you're telling me?" he asked.

"Yes."

"If you're lying, boy, I can have you shot."

I shuddered. "I swear I'm not lying to you!"

The man's face softened a little. He took a long, deep breath.

"So you love this girl?"

"Yes."

"How old is she?"

"I don't know, sir."

The man continued staring at me. A gust of wind set the leaves rustling. It was a pleasant sound, contrasting with the gravity of the situation. The man smiled sadly, absorbed in his thoughts. What would he do? Kill me or let me live? Perhaps he wanted to talk a little before lodging a bullet in my brain and burying me in the woods. The disappearance of the Vertune boy would forever remain an enigma. I shivered, thinking about Mama. She had already lost a husband; the loss of a child would be too much for her. The German captain seemed finally to believe my story. There was a glimmer of light in his eyes.

"You know, boy, I've got a daughter in Germany," he said, keeping half an eye on the other soldier a little way off.

The man clearly wanted to unburden himself, tired of fighting invisible enemies, chimeras conjured by the imaginations of the men pulling the strings of this war. The men doing the actual fighting had been obliged to abandon their families and grit their teeth as enemy bullets whistled overhead, a situation not dissimilar to when we took refuge in the farmhouse cellar as the bombs exploded outside. Though enemies, we were really not so different from each other, battling windmills like modern-day Don Quixotes. War is nothing but the bloody projection of a pained soul lashing out. Because when everything is going wrong, it's easier to hate than to love, easier to pick up a weapon than to open one's arms.

"Do you know how long I've not seen my daughter?"

"No."

"Three years. Three long years. I miss her."

"What's her name?"

"Catherine," he replied with a smile, as if pronouncing her name could somehow summon her presence.

"That's a pretty name," I said, moved by his words.

46

"It's French. My wife loved France, before all this chaos."

"I'm sorry for you," I said with a compassion that clearly touched him.

"It's not your fault. It's that Hitler," he whispered, glancing over at the other soldier.

"I know, my schoolmaster told me. His father was killed in the trenches at Verdun."

He stared at me with his blue eyes. There was a connection between us, a human link that crossed simplistic nationalistic divisions. He sighed.

"My father also died over there," he confided.

"Then why are you here?" I asked, not comprehending.

"To avenge him."

"Avenge him?"

"Yes. When war broke out, I went to the front to kill Frenchmen."

"And . . . have you killed . . . many?"

"None. I've never had the courage. And now I'm a prisoner of my revenge, when I should be with my daughter."

"What are you going to do with me?" I asked, impatient for a resolution.

"Nothing," he replied sadly.

"You'll let me return home?"

"Yes."

"Why?"

The man looked me right in the eyes.

"Your face reminds me of Catherine's. And everything that reminds me of my daughter at the moment warms my heart."

"You'll see her again, I'm sure of it."

"Do you never stop hoping, boy?"

"No."

"You better scram before someone raises the alarm. I never want to see you around here again, is that clear?"

"Yes, sir."

I got up and headed back to my bicycle, happy to still be alive, when the German officer called out to me: "Hey, boy!"

The blood froze in my veins. Had he changed his mind?

I turned to him, fear in my stomach. "Yes, sir?"

"Good luck with the girl from the farm," he said with a smile.

"Thanks," I answered, then ran to my bicycle. The German officer watched me scamper through the thickets without a word. He was undoubtedly thinking of Catherine, and his abandoning her in the hope of reconnecting with his father on the battlefield. Yet in the end he was incapable of taking anyone's life. Men can be paradoxical creatures. They strive to pursue paths of action that they ultimately find too terrible to complete, prisoners of their fears. My life would be different. Nobody would force me ever again to do anything against my will. I looked back at the Blanchart farm as I cycled away and felt a pang in my heart. Missed opportunity or valiant attempt? It all depends on how you look at it. At least I didn't have any regrets. Better to quietly wait until the war ended, if it ever did.

10

A year later, on August 6, 1944, Vannes, the nearest large town, was liberated by the Americans, who fought their way down through northern Brittany. The enemy withdrew to the east, but the war was far from over. Still, we were glad to smell the scent of freedom in our corner of the world, after four long years of occupation. Monsieur Blanchart, the mayor, had got wind of the news through official channels. We heard the joyful clamor in the village as we returned from the fields. We couldn't believe our ears. We dropped our tools and ran to join the jubilation. The men sang to the glory of the Americans, and the women danced in a circle, wearing their traditional garb, accompanied by Breton bagpipes blown by some of the older folk, who remembered the armistice celebrations of the previous war. Twirling among them was my mother, her late husband momentarily forgotten, smiling like I hadn't seen her smile in years. Every face was beaming, lit up with wide grins pulled by muscles that hadn't been used in a while. I watched this wave of fervor and I sang too, proud to belong to a great nation like France. People in the village were usually staunch Breton regionalists, but now they brandished the national flag of blue, white, and red, for when people taste liberty anew, there is no place for local rivalries or even class struggles. Everyone kissed and hugged each other, the mayor and the laborer, the grocer and the farmer.

At the center of the crowd stood Monsieur Blanchart, a proud smile on his face. For this elected representative of the French Republic, the liberation of his village tasted particularly sweet, for he had been obliged to tread a fine line during the years of occupation, continuing to oversee the local municipality out of a sense of political duty while collaborating with the Germans as meagerly as he could. Unlike most village mayors in the occupied zone, he had not resigned his post. And though he had shared power with the enemy, he had kept a watchful eye over his community and attempted to influence the occupiers' decisions as best he could. When the Germans requisitioned his barn, there was much talk of his collaboration, rumors he quashed by supplying strategic information to the Resistance, at great risk to his life. This information had enabled the Resistance to carry out acts of sabotage, which, although they contributed little to the enemy's eventual capitulation, kept alive the hope that they would eventually surrender. Monsieur Blanchart was a brave man, and the villagers knew it. I scanned the crowd for a glimpse of his daughter, but Mathilde was nowhere to be seen. Clearly she was still locked up like a nun in her cell, not allowed even to join in this day of rejoicing. My heart twinged as I thought of her.

There was a sudden disturbance in the midst of the celebrations. We heard shouts, and people began to scatter. A group of men appeared, pitchforks in hand, yowling like wild beasts. Among them were my uncle Louis and his brothers. I smiled at first, thinking they had come to join the joyful throng, but then I saw that a bunch of German soldiers were behind them, bound together and covered in blood. All eyes turned on the group. The wailing bagpipes and the singing ceased, and the women stopped dancing. The soldiers shuffled forward, heads bowed. They had clearly been beaten and dragged through the dirt. I shuddered. Was there no limit to human cruelty? Not satisfied with having conquered the enemy, it seemed my countrymen would now publicly execute a few inconsequential Nazi pawns.

My uncle pulled roughly at the rope. The soldiers collapsed together on the ground with the hoarse screams of animals being taken to the abattoir. The villagers yelled with rage, death in their eyes, demanding vengeance for those who had fallen in combat, their lives cut needlessly short. These Germans would never see their country again. They would never hold their loved ones close, smell their scents, or stroke their skin. The crowd moved in and began lashing out blindly, kicking a head here, a leg there, spitting on the soldiers and cursing at them. Monsieur Blanchart, good democrat that he was, respectful of the values of the French Republic, tried to intervene but was shoved aside. Shocked, he stared at the faces of these men and women he governed, now unrecognizable in their hate, and took a step back, terrorized. Then he turned and pushed his way through the crowd. I followed him.

After extricating myself from the heaving mass, I saw her. She was sitting on the low wall surrounding the village square, her gaze fixed on the murderous ecstasy unfolding. Mathilde Blanchart. As delectable as ever, her long hair flowing over her shoulders. I fell in love with her all over again, as if the passage of time had altered nothing, corrupted nothing. Her face hadn't changed. She was still the girl with the fair complexion I had briefly glimpsed a year earlier. When she saw her father, she waved. As soon as he reached her, he wrapped his arms around her comfortingly, protectively. Then he turned his head in my direction, clearly surprised at my apparent indifference to the surrounding pandemonium. I had eyes only for his daughter. Mathilde stared at me too, doubtless captivated by my impudence. She gave me the very first smile I was to receive from her, and I blushed. There we were, lost in each other's eyes amid the bloody chaos—a paradox of barbarism and love. Her father realized what was happening and beckoned me to come over. I did so without a word, never taking my eyes off his daughter, embarrassed at his knowing my feelings for her.

"Stay with Mathilde until I come back," he said. "Whatever you do, don't leave her!"

He ran off toward the town hall, and I found myself alone with my beloved, my cheeks as red as a beet. We looked at each other shyly, two complicated teenagers, sharing glances, neither of us daring to break the silence. And what could I have said to her anyway, a farm boy like me? Sure, I was educated, but from a poor family nonetheless. The Blancharts, on the other hand, owned land all over the peninsula. No need for them to get their hands dirty—tenant farmers like the Vertunes would do that for them. I was a little ashamed of my social status, though at fifteen years old, love is limited only by one's imagination.

Monsieur Blanchart reappeared on the steps of the town hall holding a rifle. I initially thought he intended to shoot into the crowd and take out the troublemakers, but he kept the weapon pointed skyward. A deafening shot rang out. The crowd immediately froze, as surprised as I was, and looked up at the mayor. Smoke drifted from the muzzle, spreading a pleasant, light odor of burnt powder.

"Move back, give them some air!" yelled the mayor in a tone of voice I'd never heard him use before.

"Kill them!" replied a man in the crowd.

"Move back or I'll shoot!" screamed Monsieur Blanchart.

The crowd swiftly drew back, forming a circle around the battered soldiers, who lay still.

"Don't be as barbaric as them!" he yelled. "It was a thirst for vengeance that started this war in the first place!"

"They've slaughtered our men! Now it's our turn to slaughter them." This from a woman in the crowd.

The mob began wildly beating the inert bodies again. Monsieur Blanchart fired another shot.

"Stop, I beg you! Enough blood has been spilled on our land! Go home!"

"Out of the question!" shouted another man. "They won't leave here alive!"

"Shut your mouth!" yelled the mayor.

The crowd suddenly grew silent, the villagers frustrated in their diabolic aim. Hate was written across their faces, as flushed as those of drunkards. A long moment of silence followed. As the anger gradually subsided, everyone lowered their gazes, avoiding others' eyes for fear of glimpsing the same madness. Monsieur Blanchart walked toward the crowd, sickened by the villagers' brutality. He contemplated the shapeless mass of soldiers on the ground, a tangle of arms and legs, their uniforms daubed with blood. One of them managed to raise a hand, as if to beg the man with the gun to spare him. He groveled on the ground, the strength ebbing from his smashed-up body.

I took pity on the man and rushed to help him before the villagers' astonished gaze.

"What's he doing?" asked a man, taken aback.

"I don't know," replied a woman beside him.

I took the soldier's hand. His skin was cold as ice. The man turned to look at me, his head covered in a mixture of golden hair and blood. When I saw his face, I thought I would faint. It was the soldier with eyes as blue as the sea, those eyes I would never forget, the German officer who had spared me in that forest clearing a year before, the soldier who had wanted to avenge his father but had never had the courage to kill another man. He was slowly dying, a thin stream of blood trickling from his damaged mouth. But there was still humanity in his eyes. He recognized me. His broken jaw moved into something like a smile. Comforted by my presence, he tried to speak a few words.

"Catherine . . . Catherine . . ."

"Yes," I replied, my voice barely audible.

"Tell her . . . that . . . I love her," he stammered feebly.

His head dropped again to the ground, and his back swelled with difficulty as he tried to breathe. Rasping, he managed to take a breath and choked, spitting out blood on the dirt, half suffocating. He exhaled what little air remained in his lungs, then his eyes slowly glazed over and began to close. The German officer, Catherine's father, died in front of me. He would never again set eyes on the daughter whose memory had kept him going. She would grow up without him, like my schoolmaster whose father had perished in the trenches of Verdun.

The crowd dispersed, hands stained with German blood, the blood of revenge. Monsieur Blanchart sat on the low wall that ran around the town hall, rifle in hand. He stared at the ground for a few minutes, shaken by the brutality, the cold-blooded murder of the soldiers. We glanced at each other without a word. The bodies of the soldiers lay on the ground a short distance away.

"Humanity's going to hell in a handbasket," he said, looking at his daughter.

"Yes, Papa," Mathilde politely replied.

Monsieur Blanchart stood up and took his daughter's hand.

"Thank you, Paul. Come by the house whenever you like."

His words expressed the sincere gratitude a father would accord his son. I was incredibly moved. Clearly, he saw that I had not been blinded by a thirst for vengeance that would lead me to commit the unspeakable. Mathilde also seemed moved. Her gaze seemed even deeper, more penetrating. She smiled at me again and said, "See you soon!" I blushed, my heart pounding in my chest, watching them walk away hand in hand.

The farmers began to drag away the soldiers' bodies to be thrown into a hastily dug pit and covered with earth without even a prayer or marker stone, their only company the worms that would soon devour them.

I approached the body of the German officer and crouched down. Before breathing his last, the man had entrusted me with a mission: to find his daughter and tell her that her father loved her with all his heart. He may have been my enemy, but in that forest clearing I had been moved by his sincerity, so much so that I thought it normal to do all I could to speak with his daughter. After all, none of this was her fault. Catherine had the right to know the truth about what happened to her father, and I was the only person likely to be able to tell her. But I knew nothing about Catherine. I had no address, no physical description, nothing that could point me in the right direction.

I searched the dead officer for any clues. Reaching into the breast pocket of his jacket, I found a folded card. Turning it over, I saw that it was a black-and-white photograph of a little girl, about ten years old, with a sad smile. *Catherine,* I thought. She had his eyes, the same humanity in her gaze. Was why life so unfair? All he had done was follow the orders of a tyrant whose mental health had been corrupted by the specters of his youth. And now he was dead. I too should have despised the invader, but my heart was resistant to any form of hate. On the back of the photograph was written: *Catherine. 31 August 1940. Frankfurt.* I searched the other pockets and found his ID: *Gerhard Schäfer,* it said. *Died for Germany,* I thought.

I slipped the photo into my pocket, taking care not to damage it. The officer's lifeless body was as inert and limp as the dead animals that sometimes washed up on the Breton beaches. I whispered a thank-you to him for sparing my life, and I promised to find his daughter. As preposterous and unrealizable as this quest seemed, given my financial and logistical means, I clung to this idea like a child lost in the dark searching for the light. I ran back to the farm, frightened by the deaths I had witnessed, but proud of having finally found a meaning to my life.

11

It is an implacable fact of life that everything—except, perhaps, time and the universe—has a beginning and an end. My childhood was over. Pierre had left us for two years to do his military service in Rennes. Guy was exempted for his nearsightedness. It's true he could hardly see a thing, poor kid. It would soon be my turn. Even though I hated the slightest thing to do with the army, I couldn't wait for the opportunity to leave the fields far behind and go explore my country. As educated as I was, I could only imagine the picturesque landscapes of France, the steep slopes of the Alps, the beauty of the Alsatian forests, and sophisticated Paris with its huge monuments—such a contrast to the world I'd grown up in. I was eager for adventure and discovery, like the sailor I still intended to become one day. But I dreaded moving far from Mama and Mathilde.

Things had progressed between me and Monsieur Blanchart's daughter since the day of the village's liberation. A week or so later I'd knocked on her door. Her father opened it and invited me in for something to drink. Mathilde kept us company. We spent the entire time looking at each other. I returned frequently. Her father sensed our feelings for each other and let me court his daughter, seeing in me an educated young man rather than a filthy farm laborer. After a while, he left us alone. Life is a play of resistance and acceptance, of negotiation and compromise. In this grand ball of life where we all dance to mysterious music, it is only people who change. Some resist, others give in. Monsieur Blanchart was a man of the heart who understood that objecting would serve no purpose but to fan the flames of the forbidden. And could there be a more difficult fire to extinguish? He preferred to see us happy beneath his window rather than sad and hidden in a field. Monsieur Blanchart knew a thing or two about suffering, his wife having suffered an extremely painful death a few years earlier; no need to add to it. So it was with his blessing that we strolled through the countryside, walking around the Gulf of Morbihan, and spent Sundays lying on the beach, savoring those special moments so far removed from the routine of scything and housework. Together we tasted the first fruits of love, feasting on every delightful morsel, emotional gluttons. Stretched out on the pebble beach, we wordlessly contemplated the vastness of the sea, holding each other close. Yet we never dared kiss, for fear of breaking the charm of these magic moments. I was dying to, of course, but I wanted to enjoy this carefree period—where nothing was distorted—for as long as possible.

The two years following the war were the happiest of my existence, the kind one aspires to all one's life—and that one refers to when nostalgic, to boost one's morale. I lived in anticipation of my Sundays with Mathilde, that gift sent from heaven. Mathilde was a fine seamstress and was all set to enter that profession, which she loved above all else. Often she would settle herself in the shade of the tallest oak tree in the garden and sew for hours. I would watch her in silence, fascinated by her meticulousness, noting her progress as the needle pricked in and out of the fabric. Mathilde's presence soothed the tumult of my soul. She had become a drug to which I was addicted.

My mother was no fool. Seeing her son all smiles, she could tell. But she nevertheless had the delicacy not to speak of it in front of my brothers. She was empathetic beyond belief, and I loved her for it, even though she was never able to completely fill the emotional void left by my father. Mama was one of those women who give without ever expecting anything in return.

Then there are the vampires who slake their ego with the vital energy of their victims, sucking them dry. Jacques was one of those. He grew envious of my inner strength and wanted to drill the well of my soul to enrich himself with that precious mineral. He became more attentive to me, more interested, taking advantage of the emotional abyss left by my father to weave his web. He helped me carry tools and exempted me from most of the tougher tasks in the fields. Guy, who never said anything, didn't balk when he found himself given more work than usual. He simply nodded sadly and did what his big brother told him. On Sunday mornings, just as I was leaving to see Mathilde, Jacques would pop up out of nowhere to ask for help. Often we would end up with our feet in the sludge, digging for clams all day long, like the good old times. I would think of Mathilde waiting for me in the shade of her tree, but I never dared show my frustration to my brother, for that is how vampires feast, on the fear of others, until they have totally enslaved them.

One Sunday morning, we found ourselves once again digging for clams together. It had been two months since I'd last seen Mathilde. My brother looked up at me.

"This is nice, just the two of us, isn't it?" he said, beaming.

"No, Jacques, I want to see Mathilde."

"Leave her be!" he declared with a chuckle.

A light went on in my head, sparked from I don't know where, and I suddenly understood his little game. Jacques didn't just want to be a loving brother, he wanted to keep me away from Mathilde. Lacking love in his life, he couldn't bear to see its strength expressed on my face. In the eyes of my brother that day, I saw the same cruelty as I'd seen in my father's, the same tyranny, the same desire to dominate. I dumped my tools on the ground and walked off.

"Stay here, Paul," he said in a dictatorial tone.

"No, I'm going to see Mathilde."

"Stay here or I'll make you eat dirt!" he yelled.

I turned to face him.

"Why are you like this, Jacques? Why are you so cruel, like Papa?"

"Don't you mention him!" he screamed in fury. "It's because of you he died, because of that smile stuck to your face. It's the devil's smile!"

"You're crazy," I replied, walking away.

As I continued back toward the shore, I heard Jacques's steps getting closer. His feet made a sucking sound in the soft mud. Then he leapt at me, wrapped all his limbs around me, and shoved my head deep into the mud with almost superhuman strength, fueled by the hate boiling up in him. He swore at me, hysterical with a rage I had only ever felt in my father.

"Still smiling now? I hope not!" he shouted as if possessed.

Jacques pressed down on my head with all his might, not letting me take a breath. I was trapped by my brother's weight, completely at his mercy, a prisoner of his will to crush me. My mouth full of mud, I tried to ration the final reserves of oxygen in my lungs, then began to struggle like a trapped fish. The face of Mathilde sewing under her tree smiled at me sadly. My body was no more than an envelope. I would die there, suffocated by a vengeful brother. For the second time in my life, I felt the Grim Reaper's cold breath on my spine. Then Jacques yanked my head up, I breathed freely, and Death slunk away, thwarted again. I lay on the ground, coughing up black sludge.

"That's for what you did to Papa! And don't you ever dare smile again, you hear me, or I'll shove your face into the mud until you croak!"

He walked slowly toward the shore without looking back. Then he mounted his bike, stood up on the pedals, and rode up the path from the beach. I rolled over on my back, spread my arms wide, and stared up at the sky. Large tears ran down my cheeks, mixing with the seawater from the incoming tide lapping around me. Why was life so darn complicated? All I wanted was to live out my days happily with Mathilde and be loved and appreciated by my brothers and uncles. But they were unrelenting in their jealous attempts to dampen my vibrant enthusiasm for life. I loved this land with all my heart, but I knew I had to get far away from there. I was no longer welcome in my own village, a place of desolation and sadness. I had put up with low blows, reproaches, hateful looks, and insults, despairing all the while at not being understood by my own family. But this time it was too much. The incident with Jacques was the last straw. I wanted to become the Paul Vertune I had always dreamed of being, the sailor cruising toward the horizon, weathering storms, hair blowing in the wind, and a smile on my face that nobody, not even my father or brother, could extinguish. It was time to embark for my destiny.

I turned eighteen a few days later and promptly received my draft papers for military service. I was assigned to an infantry regiment in a small town near Paris I'd never heard of, with orders to present myself as soon as possible.

Mama saw me absorbed in reading the document, with its French flag at the top, and immediately knew what it was. She stared sadly at the floor. The state was taking another of her sons away from her, and her favorite at that. I lifted up her chin. A single tear gleamed like a diamond in the sunlight streaming through the window. We hugged each other tightly and wept. I thought of all those years together, the moments of joy and pain, those magical days at the washhouse when she would pirouette in a whirl of bubbles, the smile on her lips mirroring my own, the image eternally fixed in my mind's eye. We would pick fruits in the garden every morning together, enjoying the many beautiful scents. My mother was everything to me. And now I had to leave her.

I stuffed a few things into a bag, kissed Mama goodbye, and headed up the same dirt path the priest had taken the day of my birth. At the end of the track I turned to look back at the family farm. Mama waved her arms above her head, and I sadly waved back. By the side of the farm, near the animal pen, I imagined I saw my father standing tall and smiling at me, a sincere and kindly smile I wasn't used to. He looked me straight in the eye and gestured encouragingly to wish me well in my journey far from our ancestral lands. His lips moved. He was trying to tell me something. I focused hard to decipher his words, and then I understood. My father was telling me *I love you* for the first time in his life. The image, though a figment of my imagination, warmed my heart that day, despite all the reproaches for being an inveterate dreamer that I had received since childhood. That has always been my way, fleeing the sad reality of the world around me by taking refuge within the infinite possibility of my imagination.

I headed off to Mathilde's farm to bid her farewell. She was sewing under her tree. I took her hand and explained the reasons behind my departure, the need to fulfill my civic and military obligations. Mathilde burst into tears when she realized I would be away for two whole years. I hugged her, dried her tears with a handkerchief, promised to write long letters every week and to come back for her when my military service was over. We would leave, we'd go far from this wretched village where we were both wasting away. She smiled sadly, and I repeated my earnest desire to make my life with her, to marry her. Before she had time to reply, I pressed my mouth to hers. It was our first kiss.

CRESCENT MOON

12

A few hours later, I found myself seated comfortably on a train to Paris. The steaming, smoking iron machine had intrigued me as it approached the station. I followed the lead of the other people waiting on the platform and climbed aboard, not wanting anyone to gain an inkling of my ignorance about this contraption. From my seat by the window I watched the landscape unfold before my eyes, fascinated. The train sped past fields and villages. From time to time I would glimpse silhouettes working the land, fishing by a lake, or chatting over a picnic. Some waved vigorously as we passed.

We made a brief halt at a station. On the platform stood a couple exchanging affectionate kisses. The girl was crying, the boy trying to console her as best he could. They held each other close for what seemed like an age and then he stepped away to board the train, leaving the girl distraught, weeping even harder while attempting, in vain, to wipe away her tears. It pained me to see the girl standing helpless on the asphalt, and I thought of Mathilde, abandoned beneath her oak tree. Would she have the patience to wait two whole years for me, or, unable to bear the separation, would she fall in love with the first guy to show any interest? They would walk hand in hand along the beach, set up home not far from the Vertune farm, and start a family. Mathilde would hardly recognize me when I returned. I shivered at these thoughts, and anxiety began to knot my stomach. She would never be capable of such a thing. Or would she? How well did I really know her? As honest as her father was, he might have other ideas for her, perhaps a long-planned marriage to the son of a wheat dealer or a local politician. What did I know? I was just a simple, penniless farm boy. My thoughts began to run away with me. Mathilde smiled hypocritically, hand in hand with her new lover, who was more concerned with controlling the wheat trade in the village than making her happy. The train car was packed, and I felt like I was suffocating.

"Are you all right, sir?" inquired an old lady sitting opposite me.

"Yes, madam . . . No . . . Well, yes . . ."

"Are you sure?"

I got up and wormed my way through the crowded compartment to the passageway between the two cars, stood by the slit through which fresh air was streaming, and breathed in deep lungfuls of lifesaving oxygen. My stressed body began to relax. Imagination is double edged. It can transport us to places of such intense emotion that we would happily stay there for all eternity, but it can also expose our most primal, most harrowing fears. So there I was, standing between two train cars ripping through the countryside, anguished by the images of my beloved in the arms of a fictitious husband. There was no sense to any of it. Mathilde would wait for me, of that I was certain. She was the love of my life; there was no reason to be concerned. We would await the moment when, having paid my dues of liberty to the nation, I would return to the Breton countryside and find her sewing beneath the oak in her garden as if nothing had happened.

Having calmed down, I made my way back to my seat, which was now occupied by another passenger who had taken advantage of my absence to slip his backside onto it. The old lady frowned in indignation. I remained standing and held on to the luggage rack. Outside, the green vistas had been replaced by buildings. Paris, the capital of France. I knew all the major Paris monuments by heart, Monsieur Duquerre having lent me a book on the subject. I couldn't wait to admire them laid out before my eyes and to explore this new world.

The train soon entered the station and braked with a deafening squeal that made us all grimace. When it had come to a complete stop, people grabbed their suitcases, jostling each other in the narrow aisle without so much as an apology before scampering off like rabbits hunted by a pack of dogs. They soon disappeared from view, lost in the mass of travelers gathered in this enormous station. I walked down the endless platform, a little spooked by the cacophony. People scurried in all directions, luggage in hand, shouting, cursing, and shoving. As huge as it was, the station seemed almost too small to accommodate such a crowd. I observed, fascinated, this strange ballet particular to city dwellers, the perpetual movement of bodies and objects in space, the contrasting dissonant sounds. And there was I in the middle of this choreography, the Morbihan farm boy who had never known anything but the sea breeze and the smell of wheat in the fields. We might well have been part of the same country, these Parisians and I, but we were clearly from completely different worlds.

I was filled with an urge to turn back, take the train in the opposite direction, and seek refuge in the garden at home, beneath the apple trees that had shaded me in my carefree childhood days. But that would have meant giving up. I already imagined my father greeting with me a hypocritical smile in front of the farmhouse. No, this time I would have to grit my teeth and be a man. Plucking up my courage, I forced my way through the pushing and elbowing, the shouts and the banging of suitcases crashing into each other. I had no idea where I was going. *Torcy Barracks*, it said on my draft papers. I stopped someone and asked him the way. "No idea," he replied, not even trying to understand or offering to help me find the barracks on a map.

I made my way out of the station into the cool air. The streets were huge, thick with traffic, the cars' engines throbbing and pumping out exhaust that made the air heavier than it was in my countryside.

People walked briskly along the sidewalk, looking down. Why were they all in such a hurry? Nobody stopped, they just kept on putting one foot in front of another like automatons, unlike back home, where everyone stopped to greet each other and exchange a few words. Paris was nothing like that—there was no sense of togetherness here, and it took me barely ten minutes to realize it.

The station clock showed *1:30 p.m.* I still had a few hours left to find the barracks. I decided to walk around the city a bit and set off down a boulevard, as the Parisians call these wide thoroughfares. The pale June sun barely pierced the thick clouds, but the dullness of the weather did nothing to dent my joyful mood; quite the contrary. I had fantasized about my arrival in the City of Light a thousand times as I lay in my bed at night staring up at the moon through the window, or as I toiled in the fields, bored to death.

I greeted people as I walked along, but they all seemed surprised at such attention. After a few hundred yards I reached the Boulevard des Invalides. I thought of Monsieur Duquerre with his bedraggled beard— great educator that he was, who had taught me French history. Where was my schoolmaster now? I imagined him in a high school in the Rennes suburbs, instilling the values of the Republic in his attentive pupils, who drank up his words. I didn't yet know that my poor teacher already lay six feet under, devoured by worms.

As I reached a junction, I glimpsed a gray-and-brownish structure set against the sky. I didn't recognize it at first but very quickly realized that this was the famous Eiffel Tower, the national symbol that made France the envy of the world, though few people had ever seen it with their own eyes. As I drew nearer, it slipped in and out of view behind the buildings. I broke into a run as if nothing else mattered. I wanted to see the iron beauty in all her splendor, to feast upon her with my gaze until her figure no longer held any secrets for me. Arriving at the large park, at the end of which the metal queen stood—I later learned it was called the Champ-de-Mars—I came to a sudden halt, stunned by the soaring rigidity of this unbelievable appendage to the city. It seemed to defy the laws of nature; I couldn't believe my eyes.

I sat on the grass for a few minutes, full of emotion. I felt free, happy to be there, just me and my bag packed with a few essentials: some warm clothes, underwear, photographs of Mama and Mathilde, and of course the picture of Catherine, the German girl I had to find. It wasn't much, and my back was the happier for it. Some men possess colossal fortunes, large companies, cars, houses, and goodness knows what else. Me, I possessed only the bare necessities, nothing more. It was sufficient. A person's true richness lies in their heart. I have never stopped believing this philosophy, and I would rather die than change my view.

I stood up, gave the iron lady one final smile, then set off toward the nearest street. These would be my last moments of freedom for weeks, and I savored them. As terrible as the imprisonment of the fields was, that of the army would be a real ordeal. Little did I know that inside those barracks—where a kindly chap dropped me off in his car—a twist of fate would take my life in an entirely new direction.

13

The first few months were not easy. Used as I was to the wide-open space of the countryside, it was hard to adapt to my new horizon, comprising the four walls of the barracks surrounded by forest. Being deprived of freedom has always filled me with a sense of injustice toward those in a position of authority who subjugate their fellow man on the pretext of a cause they themselves avoid serving at all costs. It was during this period of my life, locked up in the barracks, that I began to reflect upon the very principle of freedom. I had been subjected to the authority of a father who hated me, then that of a brother who'd been my ally before trying to destroy me, followed by the German soldiers, and finally my country's military. When would the time come for me to seize my life with both hands and make my own choices once and for all? Why on earth had I not, in all my eighteen years, just once been the sole skipper of the vessel of my existence? At night, when I couldn't bear it any longer, I would wait until everyone was sound asleep, then creep into the latrines and weep in silence.

We got up at five o'clock each morning and went for a run through the vast forest. Our drill sergeant, Lartigue, a veteran of both world wars, was driven by a cruel desire for domination. What horrors had he endured on the battlefield to turn him into such an abject being so devoid of humanity? He rejoiced in his absolute power, and his narcissism was unlimited. He yelled insults interspersed with orders all day long. We were completely cowed, not daring to say a single word. Even the stoutest among us—Henri, a guy from the Savoie region with whom I got along pretty well—endured the torrent of insults and the belittling of his entire family and Alpine countrymen. But what could we do? Any challenging of the state's authority would have been madness for which we would have paid dearly.

After the physical exertion of the mornings, afternoons were devoted to weapons handling. We would spend hours in the baking summer heat aiming at distant targets, constantly cursed at by Lartigue, who was never satisfied with the results. The worst shooters, who always included me, were assigned cleaning duty. Over my two years I polished miles of floor and acres of windows, toilet bowls, and sinks, and sometimes also dishes when the cook was snowed under. I spent whole afternoons on my hands and knees, exhausted by these thankless tasks. Often I dreamed of escaping that hell, but then I thought of Mathilde and reconsidered. If I escaped I would be considered a deserter and sought by the authorities, in which case it would be impossible for us to marry. I just had to grit my teeth and endure.

On our one day off per week, I wrote long letters to Mathilde. She always replied immediately, telling me about her equally boring life, the routine of a young woman stuck doing all the household chores. She would always end her letters with an affectionate phrase, such as *I miss you, Paul*, or *I can't wait to see you again*. I missed Mathilde terribly. I even had difficulty remembering what she looked like, despite the photograph she had given me. It's odd how distance sometimes effaces the dearest memories, refashioning them either through an idealizing filter or by omitting precious details.

◆ ◆ ◆

71

One October afternoon, after having flunked shooting training yet again, I found myself on cleaning duty with Henri, who, like me, spent a lot of time on his hands and knees with a scrubbing brush. Henri was a cool guy whose only aim in life was to return home to Savoie and live up in the mountains away from the busy and bothersome world. He spoke little, fell asleep as quickly as possible come evening, and made himself quite inconspicuous in spite of his imposing size, which earned him a certain mistrust on the part of the drill sergeant. He was brave but not reckless. We marched, heads bowed, toward the closet where the cleaning gear was kept, to the jeers of the other recruits—a ritual mocking of those playing the part of cleaning ladies for a few hours. Having gathered our cleaning supplies, we headed for the kitchens, which we had been ordered to scour from top to bottom.

When the cook saw us, he muttered darkly and pointed at a huge pile of dirty dishes to be scrubbed before dinner. In a corner I noticed a man I'd never seen before, a puny guy about my own age with slim features, who greeted us with a smile, in stark contrast to the foul-tempered cook. He was stirring a huge pot, with a vacant, bored air. I was just rolling up my sleeves when Lartigue entered the room and ordered us to stand at attention. We did as commanded, standing stiffly with our thumbs pressed to the seams of our fatigues. The drill sergeant walked around us, hands behind his back, wearing a serious expression. He stopped directly in front of me.

"Vertune!" he screamed.

"Yes, sir!" I replied without hesitation.

"How many times you been on cleaning duty this week?"

"Three, sir!"

"In how many days, Vertune?"

"In three days, sir!"

"Do you find that normal?"

"No, sir!"

"So why are you here, then?!"

"I'm a bad shot, sir. I'm sorry."

"*Sorry?*" he sneered. "I don't give a shit about your *sorry*. What I want is for you to be a good soldier and—"

"Yes, sir!"

"Did you just interrupt me, Vertune?!" he screamed, his eyes wide and bloodshot.

"Excuse me, sir!" I replied with fear in my belly.

"Are you giving me orders now?"

"No, sir, I just wanted to . . ."

"Shut up! Shut up, you hear me! I don't want to hear your voice again until you complete your service, Vertune, is that understood?"

"Yes, sir."

He came closer, his face now inches from mine. I could smell his foul breath, and my nose began to pucker. He seemed to sense my disgust for him. Before I knew what was happening he dealt me a blow to the stomach so violent I was glued to the spot, before crumpling slowly to the ground, eyes rolling back in my head, gasping for air. Lartigue laughed cruelly as I squirmed on the floor. It felt like my guts had been crushed. When he had had his fill of my pain, he turned on his heel and strode out of the room.

My eyes met the stunned gazes of the young man and Henri, not sure whether to leave me on the floor or to help me, wary of the drill sergeant's wrath. As for the cook, he continued as if nothing had happened, no doubt used to the cruelty administered to recruits. I gradually got my breath back. The young man came over and helped me up. I thanked him and he went back to stirring the huge pot. The urge to desert was stronger than ever, but I rolled up my sleeves and approached the sink, determined to tackle the mountain of dirty dishes. I gritted my teeth and started scrubbing. The pain shooting through my stomach forced me to stop several times.

It was late that night before we were done scrubbing the dishes, and we went to bed without having eaten more than a crust of bread. Once the lights were out, I took refuge in the latrines where, curled up in a stall, I wept and wept. I was worn out by so much revilement, tired of being so unfairly treated by other men. The light suddenly came on. I quaked at the idea of Lartigue seeing me in this state. I quietly got to my feet and waited behind the stall door.

"I know you're in there, Paul," came a gentle voice. "Open the door."

"Who's there?" I said, afraid.

"I'm the trainee cook, we saw each other earlier."

I opened the door and found myself face to face with the young man from the kitchen.

"I didn't get the chance to introduce myself. My name's Jean. Pleased to meet you."

"How'd you know my name?"

"I saw it on the meal sheet. I'm with the other regiment, in B Wing. I got here a month ago."

"I didn't know there was another regiment here."

"There's no more room in the other barracks, so they're sending us here, a few units at a time. Say, that drill sergeant walloped you pretty good in the kitchen earlier."

"I know."

"Don't worry, I've been there too. Had a few beatings myself, but I'm still alive. They're all crazy here."

"Yeah."

"Listen, Paul, I know what you're going through, it's the same for me. So if you feel like talking, I'm here. We need to stick together at times like this."

"Thanks," I said with a smile.

"OK, I'd better scram, wouldn't want anyone to find us here like this. G'night!"

"Good night."

At the door, he turned and came back.

"Say, do you know Paris?"

"No, not really."

"How about I give you a guided tour on leave day? This Sunday suit you?"

"Yes, why not," I said instinctively.

"Great. We'll leave the barracks at eight a.m., OK?"

"Yeah."

I stood there on my own for a little while longer, staring at my lean face in the large mirror. My eyes were still red from crying, puffy with sadness. The light seemed to be slowly fading in them, the optimism waning, unsteady. I was but a shadow of myself, a melancholy specter roaming the corridors of the barracks, seeking in the mirror's reflection the irrefutable proof of my belonging to the real world. I touched my face. My hands felt cold as ice. I thought of my mother kissing my dead father's forehead and recoiling, shocked by the chill of his skin. For the first time in my life, I felt scared of sinking into despair, into the dread of never being free, into madness. I would have liked to take refuge in Mathilde's arms, or Mama's, those women who never judged me, never sought to control me or torment me or bring me down, but it was impossible; they were three hundred miles away. I had to pull myself together at all costs, stop moping. I thought about Jean. I had just made a friend, or at least an ally—the definition of the word *friend* being extremely vague to me. The thought of him lifted my spirits. I went back to bed. Around me men snored, or stirred fitfully at some nightmare. *It's not all black,* I thought. *Jean seems like a nice guy. We'll see what Sunday brings.*

14

That Sunday, we met outside the barracks at eight a.m. Jean smiled when he saw me and shook my hand. We waited for Marc, a friend of his, who had offered to take us all into town. It was late October, and the sky was overcast and gray. We breathed long streams of vapor into the cold air. Jean seemed nice enough, but I remained a little wary.

His friend arrived soon in a classy little car. He seemed nice too. As we drove along, he told me that he had done his military service in the same barracks a year earlier and, like us, couldn't wait to be free of it. When I asked him what he did for a living, he replied, "I'm an actor, like him." Jean nodded and explained that they both belonged to the same theater company and that they had plans to produce their own plays together once he was done with his military service. Jean added, with a smile, that he had tried everything to get a medical discharge, from faking heart trouble to puking in front of the doctor, but none of his "performances" had yet had any success. Still, he continued to ponder the star turn that would finally pull the wool over the eyes of the medical staff and give him the liberty to pursue his passion.

Marc dropped us off not far from the Gare Montparnasse, the train station where I had arrived several months before, wishing us a good day's exploring. He would pick us up that evening to take us back to the barracks. We first went to the Eiffel Tower, which I admired for the second time, before heading to Les Invalides and its vast esplanade. After crossing the river Seine, we walked up the Champs-Élysées to the Arc de Triomphe, then turned around and came all the way back down that grand avenue to the Place de la Concorde, the Tuileries Gardens, and the Louvre, before crossing back over the river into Saint-Germain-des-Prés and then up to the Luxembourg Gardens, past the Panthéon and the Sorbonne, ending up at Notre-Dame Cathedral. It was a long walk, but I was so fascinated to discover the history of my country through these monuments that I felt I could have kept going indefinitely. Jean was an excellent guide, employing all of his actor's craft and enunciating clearly in a booming voice. He would stop in front of a monument and act the part of a king in his castle or an archbishop in his cathedral, playing each role with breathtaking accuracy. He clearly took great pleasure in telling the story of his hometown, gesticulating wildly as he narrated various characters' exploits—which I would later discover were mostly the fruits of his imagination. Now and then passersby would stop for a few moments to listen to his impassioned tales, and we would soon find ourselves part of a little group of people gathered around him, wide-eyed, lapping up his every word and applauding. He answered everyone's questions, inventing stories they all swallowed, astonished at such general knowledge. The man was indefatigable.

When I couldn't walk any farther, we sat at a café terrace on the Île Saint-Louis and chatted as we watched the Seine flowing lazily by. Weary of talking, Jean asked me about my life before the barracks. I told him about my Brittany childhood, working the fields, my dream of becoming a sailor one day, my encounter with the German officer in the forest, his death, the discovery of his daughter's photograph, and my love for Mathilde and our long walks along the beach. He listened to me attentively, interrupting only occasionally to clarify certain details. I discovered what it felt like to be the center of attention. For once, somebody on this planet was interested in me and what I had to say, and this did me a world of good. When I was done, Jean looked at me silently, simply nodding his head.

"You know that thing about the German officer's daughter, the photo you have? I might be able to help you with that."

"How?"

"Marc speaks German. He knows someone on the other side of the border. He could drive us to Germany one day, if you'd like."

"But it's impossible to travel to Germany at the moment."

"Where there's a will there's a way," he said with a wink.

"Can you really help me?"

"Yes, of course."

"When?"

"Whenever you like!" he replied with a smile. "Well, once we're done with all this and we're out of the barracks for good."

"What about you?"

"What about me?"

"What do you want me to do for you?"

"Nothing. I'm just doing it to help you." He seemed surprised at my question.

I looked at Jean's cheerful face. His features were illuminated with hope, his eyes full of kindness. It was chilly on this little Paris square, but the warmth emanating from this man wrapped itself around me, keeping out the cold. Jean wanted to help me without expecting anything in return, simply for the pleasure of helping a man who had been a perfect stranger only a week ago. I wondered what force drove this mysterious person sitting opposite me.

"So, do you accept?" he asked.

"Yes, sure, but on one condition."

"What's that?"

"That I help you too."

"That's not necessary."

"Yes, it is, at least to me. What can I do for you in exchange?"

He stared at me dubiously for a few moments, thinking.

"There's maybe one thing," he said hesitantly.

"What?"

"Help me get out of the barracks once and for all. I've got a plan."

"Will I risk a stint in the guardhouse?"

"Not at all." He smiled.

"Then I'm in. What's your plan?"

"Make me out to be a loony who has lost it from being cooped up in the barracks."

"You think it could work?" I asked, doubtful at his chances of success.

"Nothing ventured, nothing gained," he replied, all smiles. "And what's more, just between you and me, I'm a pretty good actor, so anything's possible."

Jean explained his plan to me. It was admirably simple. We would arrange for both of us to be on cleaning duty the same day. Once together, he would throw himself at me for no reason. After having demonstrated how crazy he was, he would allow himself to be restrained and would bawl like a baby, curled up on the floor, racked by a despair that no one could soothe, not even the psychiatrist at the barracks, who would examine him and also question me. I would reply that Jean had been acting strange for a while, that he could no longer bear being shut up in the barracks, and that he should be discharged as soon as possible lest things turn sour. If all went well, he would receive a medical discharge and could return to treading the boards. He and Marc would come pick me up when my own service was over and we'd head to Germany so I could speak with the German officer's daughter. Quid pro quo. A perfectly sound plan.

We sealed the deal with an enthusiastic handshake, each of us seeing the plan's benefits. We agreed to execute it two weeks later, which would give Jean enough time to get into character, according to his actor's methodology. Marc, who had just double parked across the street, approved of the plan and willingly agreed to drive me to Germany and interpret for me. He drove us back to the barracks; we entered separately so as not to draw attention to ourselves. There was no sign of Lartigue. He must have had a leave day too. Nobody could have imagined for a moment what we had planned.

The three weeks preceding our plan were the same as before, an implacable routine of sports in the morning, cleaning and maintenance duties in the afternoon, and rounds of sentry duty at night. There was nothing to upset the dreary equilibrium of our days as army recruits. I sometimes glimpsed Jean in the corridors and noted his strange conduct. Usually so jolly and extroverted, he became more withdrawn, sad, eyes staring emptily into space, his face haggard. Lartigue would set upon him, beating him violently in front of the whole barracks. But Jean remained impassive, gritting his teeth and saying nothing. He would simply get up, hang his head, and cry. It seemed like all the life had drained from him. With his pallid face, he looked like a condemned man just a few minutes from execution. On several occasions I had an urge to stand up to the drill sergeant but repressed it, not wanting to reveal our friendship and compromise the plan. So we waited patiently.

Wednesday, November 19, 1947. Some dates remain forever engraved in one's memory, triggering a nostalgic smile when one recalls them. For several days I had been deliberately aiming to the side of the target, ensuring I would be placed on cleaning duty with Jean. Lartigue, incensed at such mediocrity, had nevertheless come to accept that he would never make me a soldier worthy of the name and contented himself with screaming at me to scrub the latrines and floors faster and harder. His appearances grew rarer. That day I found myself scrubbing the barracks floor on my own. Yet again I was disappointed not to see my friend. We were now a week overdue putting our plan into effect. Perhaps we'd simply have to forget about it.

Just when I had given up hope, Jean appeared with a mop in his hand, followed by Lartigue, yelling as usual. I was shocked to see how awful Jean looked. He was a mere shadow of his former self, totally possessed by the character he had created for our purpose over the previous three weeks. I knew nothing about the theatrical arts, but the man clearly had exceptional talent. Once discharged, he would surely go on to great things in the arts world and become famous.

Jean gave me a sly wink, dunked his mop in the bucket of hot water, and began swabbing the floor. The hysterical drill sergeant screamed at the top of his voice. But when he realized that neither of us was paying any attention to his ranting, he gave Jean a massive kick in the backside, sending him flying. Jean lay on the floor grimacing and groaning in agony like a mortally wounded animal. Something in the tone of his wailing made me realize he was no longer acting. Lartigue simply yelled louder and kicked him even harder, no doubt hoping to silence his cries of pain, appearing to have lost all control. With each blow of the drill sergeant's boot, I could see the little boy humiliated by his classmates and mistreated by his parents, the teenager shunned by the girls, the young man terrorized by the bullets and shells of the battlefield and the blows of the Germans, the husband cheated on by his wife. All of Lartigue's deepest fears and inner pain seemed to have risen to the surface in a dark frenzy of violence the likes of which I have rarely witnessed. Saliva frothed around his lips, his eyes bulged in his head, and his face turned scarlet in fury. I believed he truly wished to kill Jean, who now lay unconscious, his limp body racked by the drill sergeant's kicks.

Even the most peaceful among us find that there are moments in life where something clicks and sends us over the edge. A shiver of rage rushed up my spine, the black rage of indignation that people feel when cornered, their fundamental liberties flouted. I leapt at Lartigue, knocking him off balance, and his head smacked into the floor with a dull thud. I stood there, breathing heavily, staring at the inert figure. For a moment I wanted to pummel him, smash his face, rip him apart, smear the floor with his blood. I imagined his smothered pleas, the despair and remorse gathering in his eyes as the Grim Reaper leaned in. After all, didn't I too have the right to take the easy route of violence, of cruelty, rather than always playing the sensible part? I approached Lartigue, the blood boiling in my veins, grabbed him by the collar, and raised my fist high in the air.

Right as I went to strike him with all my might, I saw the face of Mathilde covered in tears, inconsolable at the thought of never being able to hold me in her arms again. My fist stayed poised in the air, and gradually I relaxed. The hate slipped away. I let go of the drill sergeant's shirt. *What should I do now?* I jumped to my feet and realized that our plan had suffered a serious setback. Before me lay two men, completely unconscious, perhaps even dead. The situation was grave indeed. If I wanted to see Mathilde again and marry her one day, I must extricate myself from this quagmire I had gotten myself stuck in. But how? Drag the two of them into a corner and pretend nothing had happened? If the drill sergeant was merely unconscious, I'd be hauled before a court martial for mutiny when he came to. A tough prison sentence would be in the cards. I couldn't face that, nor could I face the prospect of not seeing Mathilde for goodness knows how long, if ever. I heard steps approaching in the corridor, no doubt other soldiers alerted by Jean's cries. In desperation, not knowing what else to do, I lay down on the floor and feigned unconsciousness. A few minutes later, the nurses put us on stretchers and carried us off to the infirmary. I sensed an air of incomprehension as they carried us through the barracks. A nurse lifted one of my eyelids. Would he realize the masquerade? He peered into my eye for just a moment, then let it go, no doubt wanting to attend to Jean. My mind swirled with the many imaginary scenarios that might get me out of this mess.

15

A few hours later, when I was ready to face my superiors, I called out as if I had just regained consciousness, taking care to clutch my head in apparent pain. A nurse ran to my bedside, accompanied by a portly officer of considerable rank. He sat down heavily and looked at me for a few moments. He must have been trying to deduce the truth from my appearance and gestures. Still clutching my head, I begged the nurse to give me something for the terrible pain. The officer frowned, as if doubting me. A shudder of anxiety ran down my spine. The nurse placed a poultice on my head, securing it with a bandage, then discreetly left the room. I found myself alone with the officer.

"So, Vertune, I hope you have been able to rest a little," he said in a serious tone.

"My head hurts," I lied.

"Indeed, indeed." A pause. "I am Colonel Auguste Villaret, commanding officer of this base. I am hoping you might shed some light on this . . . affair."

"What affair?" I asked naively.

"Don't you remember anything?"

"No. Nothing at all."

"You were found lying on the floor."

"What happened?" I asked, playing my role to the hilt.

"That's precisely what I'm trying to find out."

"What do you mean?" I said, acting surprised.

"You were not alone."

"Oh?"

"Next to you were lying one Jean Brisca, his coccyx fractured, and Sergeant Major Lartigue, who can't remember anything either. What the hell happened in that room?"

He looked completely flummoxed. Then I had a sudden stroke of genius. I decided to seize my chance before it was too late.

"You say that I was lying next to another soldier and the drill sergeant?" I said, pretending to recall something.

"Yes, do you remember?"

"We were on cleaning duty, weren't we?"

"Indeed you were!"

"Yes, that's it, I remember now," I said, frowning as if in concentration. "Sergeant Major Lartigue was yelling at us to scrub harder. Then he kicked the other soldier in the backside as hard as he could. I wanted to intervene but he punched me in the head, and then . . . I don't remember anything after that."

"I see," he said, unconvinced. "So you mutinied against a noncommissioned officer?"

"No, I . . . I just wanted to help my friend," I stammered, feeling like I was losing control of the situation.

"Your friend? Jean Brisca is your friend?"

"No . . . well . . . He's a barracks comrade, that's all. The drill sergeant was kicking him so hard I thought he'd kill him. I just wanted to stop him."

"I see. Jean Brisca was indeed covered in bruises, so I suppose I can believe you as far as that's concerned."

"It's the truth, sir."

84

"There's something that escapes me, though."

"What, sir?"

"Why was the sergeant major also on the floor?" He frowned.

"I don't know. Perhaps he realized he'd gone too far, got scared, and pretended to have been knocked down too?" I suggested, quite sure of myself. "I can't see any other explanation, sir."

"I see," said the officer levelly. "You are saying that Sergeant Major Lartigue lied in his statement and that he recalls perfectly well what happened?"

"I suppose I am," I said, sensing that I was now committed to my chosen path.

"You know, you're lucky, Vertune. This isn't the first time Sergeant Major Lartigue has exceeded his authority, shall we say. I don't know if your story is true, but since I don't wish news of this business to get out, I am going to believe you."

"Thank you, sir," I said, fear knotting my stomach.

"One last thing."

"Yes, sir?"

"Would you like to be discharged from military service in exchange for your silence?"

"No, sir," I replied, thinking of my brothers and the fields. "I won't say anything."

"Don't you have family or a girlfriend waiting for you?" he asked, intrigued.

"I do. But I want to complete my service, it's a matter of honor."

"As you wish. You seem like a decent guy to me. Watch out, though. Decent guys aren't too popular around here."

He stood up, nodded goodbye, and walked out of the room. I never saw him again—nor Lartigue either. We never found out what happened to him. Jean was taken to a military hospital. As he told me later with his usual verve, the coccyx is a fragile bone that takes

85

a long time to heal following violent trauma and requires extensive rehabilitation. By a quirk of fate, it was during his convalescence that he met a nurse who would become his wife a few years later and with whom he'd have two children. Our initial plan might have failed, but other paths opened, other perspectives that would never have appeared had the furious drill sergeant not lost control that day. People's lives are made up of such chance occurrences, coincidences, and choices.

As for me, I soon recovered from my imaginary head injury. When I was discharged, three days later, I found I had been assigned to the kitchens for the rest of my military service. Colonel Villaret ensured that I received favorable treatment in the barracks, having judged me to be "a decent guy." Nobody ever bothered me again. I happily assisted the cook in his everyday tasks, accompanying him to market early in the morning to buy fruits and vegetables, preparing the recipes, and so on. All in all, it was much less exhausting than spending endless days running around, crawling along the ground, and shooting at paper targets.

One day, as I was mixing fruit for a coulis, I knocked over a box of raspberries. I cursed loudly as they rolled across the white floor trailing delicate lines of red pulp. The past resurfaced, the spilled fruit evoking the garden of my childhood filled with a thousand fragrances, the branches of the raspberry bushes running along the fence, the long leaves of the apple trees waving in the wind. I saw my mother singing among the trees, arms stretched skyward, wearing her washhouse smile. I wanted to take her in my arms and waltz with her. The cook entered and swore at the sight of the fruit on the floor before getting on with his work as if nothing had happened. He preferred to hide behind his apron rather than deal directly with his fellow men, who were far too complicated for his liking, fruits and vegetables being much more docile.

◆ ◆ ◆

A while later I received a postcard from Jean thanking me and telling me his news. He had been discharged from the army upon his release from the hospital and had finally returned to acting. The play he and Marc had written had been a big hit, much praised by the critics. They were sure to become famous—it was just a matter of time. He told me they were planning our trip to Germany. Marc had a friend near Mainz who ran an inn; he had done some research on Gerhard Schäfer and come up with an address in Frankfurt. They would come get me the day of my discharge, as agreed. That was still a few months off, so as keen as I was to meet the German officer's daughter, I would just have to be patient.

I also received a letter from Mathilde telling me that her father was ill and that she was worried for his health. He was resting at home while she looked after him. I clutched the letter to my heart as I fell asleep that night. The paper still bore the scent of the Blanchart farm, and a hair was stuck to the adhesive strip. I missed Mathilde terribly. For the first time in my life I understood what a long-distance relationship really was. I came to comprehend many things about emotions during that period, how their intensity differed from person to person. The frustration of being rejected by my father, as painful as it had been, was less intense than that of not being able to kiss Mathilde. That was deeper, more invasive. I often had vivid dreams about that first kiss, and I could still feel Mathilde's lips crushing softly against my own as I wrapped my arms around her. I would awake with a start during the night, my heart racing, as my eyes desperately sought her in the darkened room. After a few seconds, I would realize that it was just a dream, a resurgence of my deepest desires. Then I would go back to sleep in my little barracks bed, my forehead beaded with sweat, filled with the anguish of her absence. Mathilde was the love of my life.

16

I stood on the sidewalk that morning, breathing the sweet air of freedom, the sun warming my skin. I glanced up and down the street for Marc's car but saw no sign of the inseparable pair of actors. I put down my bag and sat on it. Passersby looked at me curiously, particularly the kids, when they saw my shaved head.

The minutes passed, soon reaching an hour, and I began to worry. Jean had assured me they would both be here. I had difficulty believing they had changed their minds, though really nothing about human beings would have shocked me anymore. Then a large car turned onto the street, backfiring and trailing a thick cloud of smoke. People stopped and stared at the ruckus going by before being enveloped in the filthy exhaust fumes. They coughed, hands over their mouths, and cursed loudly. The car honked wildly as it approached. I saw Jean's slender profile at the wheel, his loyal companion, Marc, at his side, smiling as usual. They both waved excitedly as the car shuddered to a halt with a squeal of brakes. Jean got out of the car, ran toward me, and gave me a big hug.

"Hello, my friend!" he exclaimed enthusiastically.

"Hi, Jean!" I replied, moved at his affection.

"Excuse our lateness, but we were rehearsing all night and I didn't keep track of the time."

"Don't worry, I only just got here," I lied.

"Good. You're finally free!"

"Yes, I am."

"Great! Let's go to Frankfurt!"

We reached the German border in the early afternoon. Around us lay the majestic Alsatian forest, branches swaying in a light breeze. I thought of the French and German soldiers killed in action in these vast forests, the trees not giving a damn about our insane human conflicts. At the border post, a uniformed guard asked for our papers and our reasons for crossing. We replied that we had to visit a sick aunt, and the soldier opened the barrier and let us through. We proceeded along the roads of this devastated Germany, still occupied and undergoing reconstruction. The inhabitants looked worn out, weary of the misfortunes that had ruined their lives. They trundled through the streets, lugging bricks and bags of cement to rebuild their bombed-out homes, casting a mistrustful gaze over the French soldiers who occupied this part of the country. All that mattered to these folk was living in peace in a civilized world and never knowing war again. For several hours we drove through forests and fields, villages, and army checkpoints, without anyone stopping us. The roads still showed signs of bomb damage, three years after the war's end.

We finally arrived in Mainz around three p.m. This town on the banks of the Rhine was on the edge of the French occupation zone, twenty-five miles from Frankfurt. The American occupation zone was across the river. We parked beside an inn. Marc got out of the car and was greeted by the innkeeper with open arms. They exchanged a few words in German, then beckoned us over. We shook hands warmly with him, although I admit it was difficult to forget his nationality after all we'd been through. But that didn't seem to bother the man, who invited us to follow him inside, where he served us a copious meal. The Germans have a reputation for being generous hosts, and I discovered that that is well deserved. The innkeeper served us sausages with white cabbage, a typical dish of the region, accompanied by as much beer as we could drink. He spoke in a loud, low voice in that language whose barbaric consonants grated on me beyond measure. I listened to him politely without understanding much, since Marc's translation lagged somewhat behind the man's delivery.

When we had finished our meal, the innkeeper drove us over the Rhine. Half-drunk, he sang the whole way, the car swerving all over the road. We nearly hit the sidewalk several times, but reached the checkpoint without incident. An American soldier signaled us to stop. He approached the car, recognized the innkeeper, and waved at him, then frowned when he saw the rest of us. We handed over our papers. The soldier's frown faded when he saw that we were French, and thus allies. Jean, who had picked up some English in the Paris theater scene, explained to the American the reasons for our trip. He considered us for a few seconds, then said we could pass on the condition we return by midnight—otherwise he would have to report us to his superiors. We agreed and set off for Frankfurt at top speed.

An hour later we pulled up on a narrow street with tall houses striped in bright colors, clearly typical of the town. The innkeeper pointed at a house several doors down, and we got out of the car. As I walked toward the building where the German officer had once lived with his wife and daughter, I took several deep breaths to give me courage. Beside the door was a large panel listing all the building's inhabitants. I quickly scanned the names. My eyes froze when I saw the words: *Gerhard und Martha Schäfer.*

I pushed the doorbell for a long time to be sure it would be heard up there. Nobody came down. I tried several times more, but still nothing. Somewhat annoyed, I concluded that the inhabitants had gone out and that we'd have to await their return. Marc, who didn't want to spend all evening there, pressed the bottom bell to call the concierge. After a little while the front door opened and an old lady appeared. She looked us over warily. Marc spoke to her in German, explaining the situation. When he was done he handed her the photograph of the little German girl. Initially mistrustful, when she looked at the picture closely, her face lit up. She seemed both moved and troubled. "Catherine" she said sadly, looking up at us. I nodded, smiling at her. In a sad voice she explained, via Marc's translation, that the Schäfer family hadn't lived there since the end of the war. They had left for the Canary Islands, more specifically Las Palmas, on the island of Gran Canaria. Catherine's mother had some friends there. Upon hearing of her husband's death, she had taken herself and her daughter far away from the war and its painful aftermath. I stared at the old woman, shocked at this news, and asked her if she had an address in Las Palmas. She said she hadn't, adding that she couldn't help me any further. She wished me good luck and disappeared back into the building.

I lowered my head in disappointment. Catherine hadn't lived there for three years. The quick resolution I had hoped for now seemed impossibly distant. We returned to the car and drove back to Mainz, where, rather sadly, I thanked the innkeeper for his help and hospitality. He smiled at me sadly too, understanding my frustration, then bid us farewell.

We reached Paris sometime in the wee hours of the morning. Later that day, Jean accompanied me to the Gare Montparnasse, where, two years earlier, I had arrived in the capital for the first time.

"I guess this is where our paths diverge," I said forlornly.

"Yes," he sighed, staring into space. "Thank you for everything, Paul, I'll never forget what you did for me."

"It's I who should be thanking you, my friend," I replied, on the verge of tears.

"I didn't do much," he said with a smile.

"On the contrary. You know, this is the first time in my life that I've had a friend. A true friend, I mean, who listens to me and respects me for who I am. And for that I will always be grateful."

"One last thing before you leave."

"Yes?"

He handed me an envelope. "Here."

"What's that?"

Jean smiled. "The key to the kingdom of your dreams. Open it on the train. Have a good journey and give my regards to Mathilde."

We stood there on the platform, two faithful friends. Time seemed to stand still, the hands of the station clock halted in their relentless progress. A pleasant yet subtle fragrance of deep fellowship and affability hung in the air. We were tied by the invisible thread of humanity that forever binds those who have stuck together through adversity. The last call for the departure to Rennes echoed down the platform. I hugged Jean one last time and turned to board the train.

"Paul?"

I looked back. "Yes?"

"Don't ever lose that bright smile of yours."

I nodded and he walked away.

Thanks, Jean, I murmured to myself.

Once the train was far from the gray buildings of the capital, I opened Jean's letter.

> *Dear Paul,*
>
> *By the time you read this letter, you will probably be far from the big city. Thank you again for everything you've done for me. I would have liked to have helped you more, to pick up the trail of Catherine, but there are many unforeseen events in life. Since I have not succeeded in helping you with this particular adventure, I hope I can assist you with another one. You once told me you dreamed*

of becoming a sailor, didn't you? I enclose the address of a family friend in Bordeaux who has a shipping company. His name is Pierre Gentôme and he expects you. Go see him and he'll give you a job. There we are. May this be the start of your adventures at sea, which you've dreamt about since you were a little boy. I hope to see you again one day, my friend.

> *Fondly,*
> *Jean*

I folded the letter and slid it back in the envelope. Outside, the countryside slipped by—the many faces of France, its villages, fields, lakes, and rivers. A proud display ignored by the train as it sped past. In a few hours I would finally see Mathilde again, after waiting two long years. We would leave for Bordeaux together and I would go to sea. Destiny seemed to be smiling upon me for once. I didn't want to miss the chance of bringing joy to the face of that child who had once stared in wonder at the massive iron vessel cruising toward the horizon.

17

The sweetest summer I ever had was in 1949. The sun never stopped shining in the Brittany sky. My beautiful Mathilde was overjoyed when she saw me step into the garden as she lay under her oak tree. She kissed me tenderly and held me tight. I thought of the poor German officer who hadn't had such luck. Monsieur Blanchart, who was busy pruning his roses, also ran to greet me before discreetly stepping away so Mathilde and I could enjoy our reunion.

We walked, hand in hand, down to the coast, wandered past the little port of Logéo and lay down on the sand beside a little creek facing the Île aux Moines. We kissed and kissed until dusk's dark jaws swallowed us and all signs of human presence around us disappeared. That was the moment I knelt before her and asked for her hand. I had no ring or diamonds, but my eyes and my voice conveyed more than all the treasures of the world combined. She was quite startled at first and stared at me wide-eyed, not daring to utter the word that, once out of her mouth, would bind our two destinies for the rest of our lives. Then, having swiftly considered the consequences of such an answer, her face lit up. Her lips formed an O that became a whispered *"Oui"* that came straight from her heart, a *oui* to life and to love. Tears of emotion gathered in the corners of her eyes and streamed down her joyful face. I couldn't hold back my own tears as I beheld my future wife weeping with joy. By that creek on the edge of the sea, I understood that we were now joined forever. I walked her back home, then took the dirt path lined with brambles to the Vertune farm.

Nothing had changed there. When Mama saw me, she wrapped her arms around me and kissed me. As we held each other, I felt the intensity and depth of our relationship. Pierre and Guy got up from the table to greet me. They each hugged me, in the manner of brothers who love each other. I was surprised and touched by such a demonstration of affection. I looked at them, eyes wide, as if the sky had just fallen on my head. As for Jacques, he remained seated at the corner of the table, shoveling down food. He glanced up as I stepped into the kitchen.

"So, have you become a man, then?" he asked ironically as I sat down.

"Yes," I replied proudly, "I have become a free man."

"Free? To return to the fields?"

"I won't be returning to the fields," I declared, sure of myself.

The clink of cutlery on plates suddenly ceased. Everyone turned to look at me, surprised, as if there were no alternative in life to that miserable toiling in the fields. My mother gazed at me sadly. Long before anyone else, she had seen the desire for emancipation that had filled my soul since birth. She knew that, sooner or later, I would leave the feathered nest of conformism to thrust myself into the uncertain arena of liberty. It was my choice and she would accept it.

"And what will you do if you don't return to the fields?" asked Jacques. "Beg on the street?"

"No, I'm leaving for Bordeaux to go to sea. A friend has given me the contact of a shipping company there. I have always wanted to be a sailor, and I won't let this chance pass me by."

"What about your family?" asked Jacques, disquieted to see that he no longer had any hold over me.

"I'll come back to see you now and then. I don't want to spend my life picking up bundles of hay and scything wheat. I want to live as I wish, in my own way, that's all."

"Do as you like," said Jacques, sensing that the die was cast.

"There's something else," I said.

"What now?" asked Jacques in irritation.

"I'm going to marry Mathilde Blanchart."

Once again everyone stopped eating and stared at me, flabbergasted that the youngest of the family would be marrying, despite none of his older brothers having found a bride. Mama, in whom I had confided about Mathilde, congratulated me. All my sweet mother had ever wanted was my happiness. Had I gone to the ends of the earth to find it, leaving her behind, she would have put up with the distance in order to see me content, despite suffering terribly inside. Pierre and Guy got up to congratulate me too, although they were careful to mute the expression of joy on their faces. Jacques, his face full of jealousy, simply sat in his corner and muttered something incomprehensible. It was no longer him talking but my father, with all of his hatred—that same hatred he had passed on to my brother, who couldn't break the paternal chains, so instead played the villain. Jacques had retreated deep inside himself, and all that showed on the surface were his bitterness and resentment. But it simply wasn't my problem anymore.

To my great surprise, Monsieur Blanchart was extremely happy to learn that Mathilde and I were to wed. He invited my entire family over, but Jacques didn't come, too proud to share his brother's happiness. Monsieur Blanchart liked me despite my belonging to a social class that was usually invisible to the moneyed types who pulled the strings of the economy. I think he had seen in my eyes the same spark of passion and love for Mathilde that he'd had for his late wife. He might not have said as much, but clearly he preferred to see the flesh of his flesh marry a man who resembled him rather than some cold, dour stranger. And although it clearly pained him when I explained my intention to go to Bordeaux to become a sailor, taking his daughter with me, he said nothing.

We celebrated our marriage on Saturday, July 30, 1949. It was fiercely hot that day, and the men were all sweating buckets in their suits. The village church had been decorated with great care. My mother stood before the altar holding my hand, probably as nervous as the day she herself had gotten married in the same church, which had seen generation after generation of villagers joined in wedlock before God. Mathilde stood facing me. Through the veil covering her face, I sensed no trace of anxiety, only the deep serenity of having made the right choice, the certainty of galloping away on the right horse.

"Mathilde Blanchart, do you take Paul Vertune to be your husband, for better and for worse, till death do you part?"

"I do."

"Paul Vertune, do you take Mathilde Blanchart to be your wife, for better and for worse, till death do you part?"

"I do."

Some prayers were said; some hymns, carefully chosen by my mother, were sung. We were now husband and wife before God and our assembled families. After the church service we gathered at the town hall, where it was Mathilde's father's turn, in his role as mayor, to join us for life in the eyes of the French state. Then the entire village gathered to celebrate our nuptials with one of those feasts to which only Bretons know the secret. Buffet tables groaned under the weight of local specialties, and cider flowed like water. There was music and traditional dancing, and the women twirled to the sound of nostalgia for times past. I grasped Mathilde's waist and we danced before the guests, whirling like children in their secret garden hideaway, defying the uncertain future. We smiled at this new marital life of which we knew nothing but which appeared radiant and trouble-free. Youth has its virtues, which time patiently erodes without our realizing.

We danced until our legs could carry us no more, then we crumpled exhausted on the ground, delighted, replete with love. As the festivities continued, we sneaked away to the deserted Vertune farm, where we shared a long kiss beneath the apple trees of my childhood. Finally we undressed, excited to discover each other's bodies and to quench the desire that burned in our souls, eager to leave childhood behind and become adults. I penetrated Mathilde for the first time with infinite care. Her face suggested absolute confidence in my actions. She moaned with pleasure at my thrusting. The sky was clear, not a cloud in sight. The moon was a crescent, a heavenly smile delivered by the cosmos. Stars are not simply exploding suns, as scientists would have it, but the embers of extinguished love. They glow to remind us that, despite our lack of faith, the only thing that really counts is eternal, redeeming, sparkling love.

18

If life were a book, then Bordeaux would be a new, long chapter. The city seemed uninviting at first sight. The facades of the buildings along the river wore a thick blackish coat, as if soot had covered everything with its foul stain, marking the environment for centuries to come. The river Garonne bore a strange resemblance to the Seine in Paris: it had the same brown appearance, the same flow that seemed in a hurry to leave the city for brighter skies. There was the deafening racket of wine casks rolled across cobblestones, as heavy as the wheels of a gigantic cart, the shouts and chants of the warehousemen dexterously manipulating them, the sharp clacking of horses' hooves on the ground, and the sirens of ships as they proudly drew alongside the quay. Mathilde and I were stunned by the commercial energy of this winemaking city, by its constant assault on our senses.

Jean hadn't been lying about his friend in Bordeaux, Pierre Gentôme. The man's business was flourishing. His ships entered port packed full of commodities from overseas and set off again loaded with the products of the vineyards that filled the surrounding countryside. Monsieur Gentôme had been born and raised in Bordeaux. His family had been merchants for generations, and he was one of the most influential wine traders in the whole of the Aquitaine region. His well-respected family business dealt not only with the purchase of casks of wine from the most prestigious estates, but also handled their transportation to the port, the loading and unloading of the ships, and all of the related administrative obligations, documentation, and other formalities necessary for sale. It was a true commercial empire, managed with an iron fist by the short, bearded man I met one September afternoon in 1949.

Pierre Gentôme showed no surprise when I handed him Jean's letter. He read it and asked after Jean without seeking to find out any more about our friendship. Economic interest was clearly of more concern to this austere fellow than emotional connections. Like me, he had been raised by an authoritative father preoccupied with managing the family business. We were not so different from each other, despite our different social backgrounds—proof that money cannot replace parental love. He asked me if I knew how to read and write, then seemed surprised when I replied in the affirmative, as if it had never occurred to him that fate might have given me the chance to escape the constraints of my social status. He shrugged and handed me an administrative form to fill out, which I did meticulously. Monsieur Gentôme watched as I did so, no doubt to test the veracity of my claims. This embarrassed me. As the interview reached an end, he extended a limp hand and welcomed me to his company. I was given the job of a warehouseman, or *stevedore*, as everyone called it. He showed me around the premises and introduced me to several of his other employees, who greeted me with all the warmth that the working class reserves for a new colleague. Monsieur Gentôme explained that, like all novice stevedores, I would join the twenty-strong night shift led by a foreman who would show me the ropes. I was to start the next day. Then he headed back to his office, having devoted enough of his precious time to me.

◆ ◆ ◆

Not long after that, Mathilde and I set up home in a working-class district of Bordeaux, west of the Garonne River. It was a single-story house with a small garden where we grew a few fruits and vegetables.

At first I was worried whether Mathilde would agree to such a modest dwelling, having lived in a huge farmhouse since she was a child, just she and her father. For my part, I was used to living in small quarters, having shared a room with three brothers. But Mathilde was delighted to be moving in with me, and wasn't bothered by our humble abode, nipping all my concerns in the bud. We concluded that the house was sufficiently large to contain the few possessions we had between us. Besides, our finances would not permit us to rent anything more spacious. "Let's worry about comfort later," we joked to each other. Besides, we really liked the neighborhood. It was mostly inhabited by laborers and stevedores who, like me, worked hard and unrelentingly to elevate the city of Bordeaux. We soon became friends with several local families.

As the months passed, we got to know our new environment inside out, the particularities of the various shops and boutiques, and local customs and bigwigs. Mathilde developed a friendship with Joséphine, our next-door neighbor who was also the local baker. She introduced Mathilde to a family acquaintance, Madame de Saint-Maixent, an upper-middle-class lady from a family that had made its fortune trading luxury fabrics, and who idled away her lonely days in a house that was far too big for her. She hired Mathilde officially as a full-time seamstress, cleaner, and nanny to her children. Unofficially, Mathilde kept Madame de Saint-Maixent company, served her tea, read her the newspaper, patiently taught her needlework, and looked after her children with such kindness that she soon became indispensable to the family's fragile equilibrium. My wife, as conscientious as her mother had been, worked hard and came home late in the evening, worn out from her long days but satisfied at having contributed to our income, even though Madame de Saint-Maixent paid her meanly for her good and faithful services.

The first two years of our Bordeaux life flew past. By the time Mathilde came home in the evenings, it was time for me to leave for the docks, where I spent the night loading ships before returning home in the early morning, just as Mathilde was heading out to work. We saw very little of each other except on the weekend, when we were able to enjoy those privileged moments when life gives you a short respite.

My job as a stevedore was exhausting. I hadn't found it difficult at first—quite the opposite. Night work offered considerable advantages, such as being able to enjoy sunset and sunrise while the city slumbered. The pay was more than generous, and I got the whole weekend off. But what was really important to me, though most mortals would find it strange, was being able to contemplate my sweet moon up in the sky whenever I wished. The sight of it brought back so many memories of my childhood in the Brittany countryside, and it lifted my spirits on those nights when the port was thick with ships vying for our attention. For a while I was quite content with my lot—happy, even, despite the little time I got to spend with my wife.

But then the work grew tedious and mind-numbing. My body soon became prisoner to this nocturnal hell punctuated by the sirens of the ships and the chants of the stevedores, the nights growing ever colder as winter drew in. We rolled cask after cask of wine across the ground, handling them carefully so as not to spoil the precious nectar contained therein, before stepping into the bowels of the iron beasts, which berthed at dusk and left early the next day, fully loaded, for a distant destination I knew only from the world map my schoolmaster had pinned to the wall. When I left work early each morning, I would watch the ships sailing out of port, zigzagging between the sandbanks of the Garonne estuary, and my heart was heavy as I saw them disappear from view, thinking of the sailors happy to be heading for distant lands.

My childhood dream remained intact. Deep down I couldn't wait for it to finally become a reality. I never lost hope of one day being part of a crew and seeing the tropics. To console myself, I returned home to the bed still warm from Mathilde's body. And there I fell asleep, sheltered from the din, dreaming of wide-open spaces and paradisiacal landscapes.

19

Three years passed in this way, me busy at the docks, Mathilde managing the caprices of Madame de Saint-Maixent. But one morning in 1952, destiny knocked at my door again. Is there an ingredient list for that dish called coincidence? A particular combination of places, moments, people, planetary alignments? Whatever it was, a magical cocktail of all these ingredients suddenly came together that day and changed everything.

I was about to leave the deck of a ship we had just loaded when a noise behind me made me jump.

"Pssst, over here!" whispered a voice.

I turned around but saw no one, only a heap of rusty containers. Looking over the guardrail, I noticed a woman in the prime of life waiting on the quayside, her arms crossed. She seemed troubled. Her face was lined, and the deep, dark bags under her eyes were laden with a despair she had difficulty masking. Her hair was pulled back into a hastily gathered ponytail that itself seemed to sum up her psychological setbacks.

"Young man," came the voice again.

From the heap of rusty containers, a head appeared. A thick black beard covered most of the man's face. Like the woman down on the quayside, he also seemed quite troubled.

"Come closer," he whispered, barely audible.

"Me?" I asked, surprised.

"Yes, you! Hurry up, come here!" replied the man, irritated.

I approached him cautiously, wary of finding myself face to face with a complete lunatic. When I was a few yards away, he beckoned me to join him behind the heap of containers. I did so and beheld a hefty man wearing a navy-blue uniform. There were several stripes of braiding on his shoulders and a variety of colored medal ribbons on his chest. He must have been a highly placed officer, a fearless sailor who had confronted countless gales and angry oceans. So why was he hiding behind this pile of containers like an escaped convict on the run?

"You have to help me, young man," he implored.

"Help you? To do what?"

"To hide!"

"Hide from what?"

"From the woman down there on the quayside. Did you see her?"

"Yes, I think so. The one waiting with her arms crossed?"

"Exactly! You have a good eye, kid, it's a fine quality! Now, listen to me closely. She mustn't come aboard this ship, do you understand?"

"Why not?" I asked, intrigued.

"Just do what I tell you. I'll explain afterward!"

"All right. What should I do?"

"Block her way when she tries to come aboard."

"And if she stays down there?"

"If she stays down there you've got nothing to do."

"OK," I said, not understanding what on earth was going on. "And what should I tell her, exactly?"

"Tell her she can't come aboard because of a contagious disease, a virus brought back from the Canaries."

"The Canary Islands?" I wondered aloud, thinking about the German officer's daughter, Catherine.

"Yes, the Canary Islands, need me to draw you a picture?"

"No, no . . ."

"Well, then. Stand on the gangway and block her way until she leaves!"

"And what's in it for me?"

The words shot instinctively out of my mouth. The man seemed disconcerted by the question, as if the power balance had shifted in my favor, something he wasn't used to. After all, it was he who needed me, not the other way around. He stiffened his back and looked me straight in the eyes for a few seconds. Then he took a step toward me. The alcohol on his breath tickled at my nostrils.

"If you get me out of this fix, kid, you can ask me for whatever you like," he declared.

"Very well," I replied, satisfied with his answer.

I made for the gangway and began to walk down it carefully, my feet pressed to the wooden ridges that prevented one from slipping on the steep incline. The woman was still standing at the bottom of the gangway, arms crossed, watching me with furious eyes. As I descended, I began to imagine a plausible scenario between these two characters in the vaudeville we were now all three engaged in. I decided that the woman was either one who had been cheated on, or else the disillusioned lover come to bawl her distress to whoever might hear, kicking up a scene in order to blight the image of her sailor sweetheart. A clash seemed inevitable either way. When I was a few yards from her, she uncrossed her arms and seemed to transform into a viper trying to infuse me with the toxic venom of her words.

"You there!" she said coldly.

"Yes, madam?" I calmly replied.

"Go fetch me the ship's captain!"

"For what reason, madam, if you please?"

"For the reason that I am his wife and I want to see my husband." Her voice quivered with anger.

"That's impossible, madam, I am sorry."

"What do you mean, impossible?"

"The ship is in quarantine and the whole crew is stuck inside," I lied rather unconvincingly.

"In quarantine? I don't believe you!"

"I have orders not to let anyone through. This ship is infected with a virus brought from the Canary Islands, a highly contagious virus carried by rats," I improvised to heighten the fear of possible contamination.

"Oh, really? What virus?" She was having none of it.

"We don't know yet. In the meantime, nobody is allowed on board."

"That's yet another two-bit excuse dreamed up by my husband, isn't it?"

"I have no idea what you're talking about, madam, I'm sorry."

"Yeah, right. You're all the same, a bunch of dirty liars."

"No, really, I—"

"Just tell him I know everything! If I see him again, I'll kill him!"

"Calm down, madam, please."

"I'll kill him, you hear me? I'll kill him!" she screamed before collapsing to the ground.

She began crying hard, her face a twisted mask of rage and disappointment. Holding her head in her hands, she mumbled something, no doubt cursing the man who had caused her so much pain. She wept harder—heavy, meaningful sobs that seemed to come from the depths of her soul. Little by little I felt myself overcome by the immense despair of this cheated creature. Had I just been turned into the devil's advocate? What kind of individual was he? A coward? How could a man who steered a ship across the waters of the globe be so scared of his wife? To my great surprise, I had discovered another paradox of humankind. I knelt beside the weeping woman and tried to help her to her feet.

"Leave me alone! You're a liar, too, like him!"

"No, really, I—"

"I thought he was a good man. Look at me now, I'm waiting on this filthy quay while he's with his mistress. I'm desperate," she murmured between sobs.

"Not at all, madam. Please get up." I didn't know where to begin.

"Leave me alone, or better still, throw me into the sea, I want to die," she implored, crawling across the ground.

"Stop!" I yelled, grabbing hold of her with all my might.

"Let me die!"

All eyes on the port were now turned in my direction. I hung on to her, praying that someone would come help me, for the now completely hysterical woman was beginning to wriggle free of my grasp. For a moment I imagined what the watching stevedores and sailors must be thinking. I was scared they would take me for a lunatic attempting to rape this poor, struggling woman. I thought of Mathilde, my love, who would probably have been shocked to see me in such an outrageous position. I yelled for help, for someone to help me reason with this desperate woman who seemed ready to do anything to cease the suffering that was eating away at her. The stunned bystanders suddenly shifted out of their lethargy and came running. One of them grabbed the woman, allowing me to finally loosen the grip that was killing my hands. Once she had been entirely immobilized, she gave up and went limp on the ground. Her anxious husband observed the scene from the ship, clearly alarmed by the brutal treatment his wife had received. But he did nothing, no doubt seized by guilt, a spectator to the emotional degradation of his marriage: all those years of life together swept away by the desire for something new, for "fresh meat," as sailors would say. The woman, now smeared with patches of black grease from the quayside, had stopped crying.

The swarm of bystanders gradually melted away, folks sarcastically remarking about the poor woman and her pain. But she seemed not to hear anything. Her spirit, broken by sorrow, had switched off. I quietly sat down beside her and contemplated the brown waters of the

Garonne. Its flow carried all sorts of detritus in its long marathon to the ocean. Occasional objects would bob to the surface, and I recognized a shoe and a bicycle frame. Sometimes whole animal carcasses would float past like broken puppets. We both sat there, the cheated wife and the farm boy far from his fields, staring into the void of our lives.

The silence became oppressive and I felt that the woman wanted to open up. She told me the story of the captain and their marriage, which was no more, ever since she'd discovered his mistress's torrid letters to him, that same husband who was watching us from the ship's guardrail, concealed in the shadows. Whenever he was in port, the wife told me, the captain would entertain his mistress in his cabin. In that enclosed space smelling of the sea, they would indulge in all sorts of erotic games to which his wife only alluded, out of modesty. For a moment I pictured the old captain in his cabin, completely naked save for his bushy beard, chasing his mistress with a whip in his hand. I dismissed the abominable image from my mind.

A few minutes later, having fully unburdened herself, the woman thanked me kindly, got up, and staggered away, befuddled with sadness and disillusionment. I watched her leave with a heavy heart, aware that I had covered for the captain's sexual indignities with my lies, I who was as faithful in love as a dog was to its master. I walked sadly back up the gangway, dragging my feet, crushed by guilt. On the ship's deck, I found the captain sitting against the guardrail wearing a hangdog expression. *What a craven fellow,* I thought, going to sit next to him. We said nothing for a long while.

"Thanks," he said quietly, staring down at the deck.

"It's nothing," I answered automatically.

"My wife has a tendency to exaggerate," he declared, seeking to exonerate himself for his atrocious acts.

"Perhaps. I don't know."

The captain stroked his beard.

"Life's complicated, kid. At your age, you figure everything's easy and will always remain so. But you're wrong. Everything becomes complicated and sad. Time passes without you noticing, and then one day you wake up. You look at yourself in the mirror and see that your face is covered in lines. It has changed, aged. The face that looked back at you thirty years ago, when it was young and full of hope, has disappeared, evaporated, dissolved, just like your dreams. And when you realize that, all you can think about is reverting to what you once were."

"So you cheat on your wife?" I asked, gazing into space.

"I couldn't help myself. When I saw Patricia, I glimpsed the face of the young man I was thirty years ago, without wrinkles or scars, reflected in her eyes. I was unable to resist the call of youth."

"And what do you see when you look in your wife's eyes?"

My question disturbed him.

"I see myself old and ugly, abraded by time."

"And what does that image evoke?"

"Death."

"Are you frightened of death, Captain?"

He lowered his gaze.

"Yes," he replied.

A tear formed in the corner of the old man's eye, a tear that spoke volumes about his ability to contain his emotions, to bury them deep inside himself. Why the hell was all this so complicated? The mystery of life floated above our heads, above the ship, the region, the country, the whole world. There we were, devoid of experience despite the many years between us, simply fools whose only hope was to one day crack the secret of existence.

"I told you earlier that you could ask me for anything you wanted if you got me out of that tight spot," the captain continued.

"Yes," I replied, lost in my thoughts.

"I'm listening . . ."

In my mind's eye, I saw the figure of the sailor at the port of Arzon twenty years before, his smile when he placed his cap on my head, the childhood dream he had triggered in me. Then came the image of Catherine Schäfer, her dead father, the trip to Frankfurt with Jean, the smile on the face of the concierge as she looked at the little girl's photograph. It all came back to me. The captain had mentioned the Canary Islands a few minutes earlier, those same islands where Catherine's mother had fled with her daughter upon learning of her husband's death. All the puzzle pieces of my existence began to spin, twirling above an imaginary table, then interlocking one by one, first the corners, then the sides and the center, until everything was perfectly joined, aligned, significant. I turned to the captain and solemnly declared, in a confident voice: "I want to become a sailor too."

At first the captain couldn't believe his ears. He looked at me, amazed, as if dealing with a lunatic who had drawn no lessons from the drama that had just played out before him. He sighed, his body exhausted by all those years at sea, steering a course between icebergs, fighting against storms and deadly waves and other unbridled elements of nature that would never allow themselves to be tamed. Then he questioned me about my decision, asking how much I really knew about this profession—the toughest there was, according to him. He wanted to understand my motivations, to detect if this was no more than the passing whim of a young man hungry for adventure. When I told him briefly of my childhood memory, those bizarrely dressed strangers who had suffused me with this crazy dream, he smiled and conceded defeat. There was clearly nothing more to be done. A childhood dream is a perfectly oiled machine, which nothing and no one can obstruct, particularly in those who faithfully await their turn without rushing or wearing themselves out in vain.

The captain thought for a little while, frenetically stroking his beard as if this were the decision-making part of his coarse being. Then he stood up, extended a hand to help me to my feet, and agreed to enlist me on his ship, the *Volcan de Timanfaya*. He explained that the company that chartered his ship specialized in trade with West Africa and Asia. His routes took him to places like Bordeaux, Lisbon, Tenerife, Las Palmas, Abidjan, Durban, Bombay, Singapore, and Saigon. Apprentice sailors usually started out on the shortest routes in order to test their capacity to put up with separation from their families, as well as seasickness. After a few years, once they had built up enough experience and proved themselves, they would switch to a large freighter carrying considerable tonnage to more distant ports. They would see a significant rise in their salary but would spend much more time away at sea—sometimes over six months, which put off some sailors who feared the effect on their families. A sailor's life was a strange paradox, the captain said, a conflicting mixture of frustration and freedom, where it was impossible to strike a balance. But it was exactly this mix that made sailors feel alive, he added with the air of a Greek philosopher. It was a hard job, he concluded, because one felt constantly frustrated at not seeing one's children grow up, not being able to embrace one's wife. But it was a rewarding profession that opened up the world, providing the opportunity to spend hours watching sea life and the sumptuous passing landscapes. He said he wouldn't give up this sense of freedom for anything in the world. He thanked me and disappeared through a door that led off the deck into the steel colossus that would soon be my traveling abode.

I hurtled down the gangway with a light heart. As I walked home I thought of my mother, singing to herself in the mornings as she picked fruit in the family orchard. I began to hum one of her tunes. My father would have been proud of me, I told myself without being totally convinced. I quickened my step home. I couldn't wait to tell Mathilde the news.

20

Three weeks later I prepared to embark aboard the *Volcan de Timanfaya* for the Canary Islands.

Pierre Gentôme didn't seem surprised when I handed him my resignation. He merely shrugged and wished me good luck. However, before I left he added that his door remained wide open, should I ever change my mind. As for Mathilde, when I first told her, she burst with joy and pride at the idea that a high-ranking captain wanted to hire me for his ship. Her enthusiasm waned somewhat when she realized that I would have to spend several months a year at sea. It was as if she hadn't realized that absence was one of the key characteristics of a sailor's profession. As long as a dream remains just a dream, one doesn't properly gauge what it requires of us.

Nevertheless, my new status gave me a few firm benefits. For each month spent at sea, the company would grant me two weeks' leave, during which I would be free to spend as much time with my wife as I wished. The lowest pay grade was twice as high as that of a stevedore at the docks. Mathilde and I used the extra money to buy a house not far from where we had been living. Since we had already set up home in this new city, and in a neighborhood we liked, we wished to minimize any more disruption to our lives. Before I embarked, we held a party to celebrate my becoming a sailor. All my neighbors came to congratulate me on this position, which so many men coveted without daring to go for it. No doubt this indecisiveness owed much to their wives' fierce will to keep their husbands close by.

It was the day of my departure, my giant leap into this masculine world tossed on the ocean waves. Mathilde and I were both edgy as we got up that March morning, gnawed at by the fear of not seeing each other for a month. I would never have forgiven myself if something happened to Mathilde while I was away. For several long minutes I felt like giving up on the idea and just snuggling closer to my wife, making love to her, then falling asleep by her side, cozy and warm beneath the eiderdown, where we'd be safe like two kids in their playhouse at the bottom of the garden. After all, Mathilde was the love of my life, the girl who had made my heart beat faster from the first moment our eyes met. I sat on the edge of the bed with my head in my hands. What should I do?

I imagined the ship leaving port. *A long column of smoke rises into a sky full of seagulls screaming my name:* Paul! Paul! Paul! *I stand on the quayside, my eyes full of tears. The captain leans on the ship's guardrail, laughing through the mist at my indecisiveness. My father appears beside him, takes his arm, and leads him in a ritualistic dance to the accompaniment of the screaming gulls:* Little girl! Little girl! Little girl! *The pair are soon joined by a cohort of exuberantly tattooed sailors, and they all dance, arms linked, in a sort of diabolical cancan. I crumple to the ground, weary of being a little girl, weary of not being able to accept my choices, weary of hesitating. The ship disappears into the mist, leaving behind nothing but silence.*

I realized how difficult it is to attain one's childhood dreams, and how hard it is to remain focused on one's goal. Life constantly offers us newer, easier, less restrictive paths. We turn down them with disconcerting ease, like a herd of cows being led to the slaughterhouse. But I wanted to see things through, to satisfy that little boy on the quayside with his sailor's hat, to wipe the mocking smile off my father's face and make the two women in my life, Mathilde and Mama, proud.

I stood up from the bed, possessed by an invisible force, a mixture of anxiety and exaltation. Mathilde got up too. She looked nervous. I faced her and told her I loved her and that she had always been the only woman for me and always would be. But the little boy inside me couldn't wait any longer; he demanded his slice of the pie. He wanted to live, love, escape, feel, travel, explore, imagine, learn, marvel, play, smell, taste, touch, hear, see, open his arms to destiny, and embrace life fully. He had to leave. Mathilde watched me dress, eyes wide, as if a ghost had appeared to haunt her. I took her in my arms to reassure her. My excitement at starting this new adventure made me feel almost crazy. I was filled with the kind of true happiness that makes your heart beat faster and gives you the strength to move mountains.

Mathilde accompanied me to the ship, subdued. I promised to write her letters and mail them as soon as the ship reached port. She smiled shyly, wiping away a tear with the cuff of her sleeve. My beloved. My Mathilde. My other half.

At the port, a group of men and women had gathered close to the gangway leading up to the massive ship. Its engines began to throb in the harbor. At its stern, huge bubbles formed in the water, emerging from the depths like a geyser spurting from the belly of the earth. The men on the quayside, used to this ritual, comforted the weeping women, who were tired of being abandoned. Here in this sizable port, couples formed and split according to the rhythms of shipping and the huge profits reaped by owners who, ensconced in their comfortable apartments, never had to deal with such frustrations. Inequality is emotional as well as material. Some grab all the joy and happiness while others, through an accident of birth, must make do with sadness and frustration.

I wrapped my arms tenderly around my wife and kissed her forehead and cheeks. I told her again how much I loved her. Nothing and no one could change that. Neither the ocean nor the distance would ever remove the faith I had in our union. I kissed her lips, thinking of my marriage proposal by that little Brittany creek. My sweet thoughts were rudely interrupted by the sound of the captain's whistle. I let go of weeping Mathilde, picked up my pack, and headed up the gangway. A river of tears poured onto the quayside. The men climbed aboard while their women waved tear-soaked handkerchiefs above their heads. This was the great moment of departure, the one I had witnessed twenty years before in wonderment without realizing that sailors' veins are filled with rivers of sadness. I shouted passionate "I love yous" to Mathilde in farewell. She waved her arms wildly as if she had never known shyness, shattering the decorum taught by her parents, shucking off the demanding habits and customs that constrained her, that constrain us all. For a moment she became the little girl she had ceased to be when misfortune had struck her family and carried off her mother forever. She was soon a little black dot on the horizon, dwindling until I could see her no more.

The countdown had begun. A month without my wife. The ship's siren blared loudly across the deck. The captain had the decency to wait until we had said farewell to our weeping women before addressing us, he who cheated on his wife without a second thought. But he was in charge. The old, experienced sea dog had the mission of sailing between two cities that lay fifteen hundred miles apart. The time for reflection was past. We had to prepare the ship for when the ocean waves started slamming against the hull, trying their utmost to capsize us. He strode about yelling orders left and right, reminding sailors of their tasks.

"Dhenu and Bonnarme, galley!"

"Yes, Captain!"

"Bouquet, engine room!"

"Yes, Captain!"

"Ducos, bridge!"

"Yes, Captain!"

Then he turned to me, thought for a few moments, and ordered me to follow him. We entered a narrow passageway and proceeded through a labyrinth of mazes, hatchways, and corridors. I soon felt like I'd been plunged into a story from Greek mythology. Like Theseus pursuing the Minotaur, I followed the master of the house through the tight spaces of the steel hulk. The captain halted in front of a door, opened it, and signaled that I should leave my pack there. My cabin: two bunk beds on either side, along with four tiny lockers. I threw my pack down, and the captain closed the door and handed me a key.

We returned to the labyrinth. I felt swallowed by the passageways, which were all painted the same dark green. The captain stopped before another door, opened it, and took out a mop and bucket. He told me to go swab the deck. The vague memory of the Torcy barracks returned to haunt me: those endless hours spent scrubbing the floors, cleaning the disgusting toilets, the windows, the cutlery, and the dishes. "We all start like this," the captain said, appreciating my lack of interest in household chores. He gave an ironic smile and disappeared down the maze of corridors without waiting for me.

I took my charwoman's tools and headed for the deck, trying to backtrack the way we'd come. I took the wrong passageway several times, returning to my starting point, before the lights suddenly went out and I had to fumble my way along, unable to find the light switch. I was completely lost. Several sailors rushed past, preoccupied with their work, in that state of constant alertness you have to adopt at sea in order to survive. I tried to ask one of them the way. They laughed and ignored me. After several more fruitless attempts, I finally managed to reach daylight, which I found dazzling after wandering around in the dimness below deck. When the other sailors saw me, they applauded in unison. The captain stepped forward and warmly shook my hand. He explained that all this was an initiation ritual, a way of tightening the bonds between crewmembers. "You have to lose yourself to find your way. That's true both aboard ship and in life," he said, launching into a series of scandalous anecdotes about his adventures—both maritime and erotic—while roaring with laughter, proud of doling out his philosophy to the sailors under his command. He wasn't wrong. Life is a huge ocean liner carrying us all. We open and close doors according to our moods. Some people reach rock bottom before they see the light. Others, weary of contemplating it, throw themselves over the guardrail, dissatisfied at not being able to discover more, preferring to explore the depths of the sea at the risk of drowning themselves. Still others wander their whole lives in the bowels of the vessel, scurrying to find the exit, thrown around in the passageways by the buffeting of the swell. The path to truth is not a straight line.

A week passed quickly. I tirelessly scrubbed the bridge, rubbing hard to remove the salt deposited by squalls. It was not an easy job, as I quickly realized. But I held fast to my dream like a lioness holds fast to her cubs. At night, while most of the ship's company slept, and when the sea was behaving itself enough to let me go outside, I would stretch out on the deck and stare up at the sky with its infinite blanket of stars. I was happy lying there like that, as I had been in the garden as a child. The moon shone in the sky, illuminating the ocean with its soft light, changing over the days as its position shifted, from smiling crescent to tranquil quarter to full and melancholic, but always with the same intensity of gaze, the same ardor, the same perpetual exuberance. Watching this celestial extravagance, I secretly prayed that nothing would wither: my love for Mathilde, for Mama, for my whole family. I prayed for life to be simply an ocean of tenderness, a calm lake on which my craft would cruise freely. When I reached my peak of relaxation, there on the ship's deck that was my planetarium, it appeared in all its splendor. I saw it. Yes, I saw it. The smile of the moon . . .

QUARTER MOON

21

A week later, we reached our first destination, Las Palmas de Gran Canaria. It appeared on the featureless horizon as if by magic, a dark speck that became a looming mass as we approached, a jutting promontory surrounded by the Atlantic Ocean. The sky began to fill with seagulls screeching in their incomprehensible tongue, many of them gliding to perch on the ship. I was astonished at the contrast between the deep-blue ocean, the dark rock, and the azure sky. And there was the sun shining high above, bathing the whole landscape in its golden light. The panorama seemed unreal, like something straight from the imagination of a painter whose brushstrokes had no limits.

"It's beautiful, isn't it?" the captain murmured in my ear as I stood there on the ship's bridge.

"Yes, Captain," I replied, gazing at the horizon.

"I've been sailing these waters for thirty years and I still get dazzled by the beauty of the Canary Islands," he added.

Motionless, we stood there for a while, hypnotized by this sublime, timeless scenery. There are few things, few moments, few places that move a man to this extent. We were in perfect harmony with nature, the captain and me, our souls filled with a serenity that cannot be altered by any terrestrial cares or concerns. All was beauty and hope.

Yet the crossing had not been entirely serene. We had been hit by a gale off the Portuguese coast that had confined me to my bed for an entire day, puking into a bucket, struck with a seasickness I hoped never to experience again. The feeling of pitching with the swell soon became unbearable. Several times I felt like hurling myself out of my cabin's porthole just to make it stop, to regain a little stability in that constantly shifting world of the open sea. Seasickness is an ordeal in which one curses the natural elements gathered to remind us that, despite our arrogance, we are simply guests at Mother Nature's feast.

I shared my cabin with three other sailors—two Frenchmen and one Spaniard—and the cramped space was devoid of any comfort. "You don't go to sea for privacy," sniggered one of the Frenchmen, with whom I had attempted to strike up a conversation without any success. The other Frenchman didn't talk much either. The Spaniard, who answered to the name of Martín—pronounced *marteen*—was much more talkative. In comparison to him, the French sailors appeared sad and uninteresting. Martín spoke perfect French and expressed himself with that marked accent Spaniards have, in which they pronounce all the letters of their language. He talked very, very loudly, waving his arms around to illustrate his points and cursing profusely, which wasn't to everyone's taste. He would say *"Ay amm Marteen ffrom Andaloussiaa"* to remind us how proud he was of his country of birth. Sometimes, when he had drunk too much, he began dancing on the table, clicking his fingers above his head and striking the wooden top sharply with his heels. Everybody laughed and applauded. Martín was one of our only sources of entertainment, truth be told. We were bored stiff whenever he wasn't around.

One evening, when it was just the two of us on deck, Martín told me his story. He had an extraordinary way of recounting his existence, alternating tragic tales, which had me oozing compassion from every pore, with comic interludes that had me in stitches. He lampooned some of the more awful episodes of the Spanish Civil War, doing a wonderful imitation of General Franco and his hatred of the Communists—the scapegoats of the regime. Martín talked and talked, never tiring, while I listened, like a little boy on his grandfather's knee. In his words I detected a constant faith in human nature and an unconditional love for others, coupled with an intense lust for life. When he had finished his story, I told him mine. He didn't interrupt once, a sign of great empathy, in contrast to more egocentric folk who are always butting in—and with whom I've always had great difficulty in forging links. I told him the story of the German soldier, his tragic death at the hands of my fellow citizens, my expedition to Frankfurt only to discover that his daughter had gone to the Canary Islands, how I'd become a sailor. His eyes suddenly lit up when he realized the connection between my story and our current destination. It touched something in his romantic nature, and he offered to help track down Catherine Schäfer. We would get a few days' shore leave when we moored in Las Palmas before making the return trip, giving us plenty of time to pursue our investigation.

And that is what we did as soon as we stepped off the boat the following morning, as dawn was breaking.

"Where shall we start?" I asked.

"At the *ayuntamiento*," answered Martín as if it were the most obvious thing in the world.

I was a little embarrassed. "The what?"

"The *ayuntamiento*, the town hall. It's this way."

We walked through the port, scattering seagulls, past stevedores hard at work unloading the ships, singing loudly to keep up their morale, a practice that must be the same the world over. Beyond the port we could see the town, each house painted a different color. One was mauve, another yellow, another red, another blue, as if a building's color denoted the inhabitants' social status. *Odd custom*, I thought, although I wasn't sure if wealth really had anything to do with it. Two huge mountains overlooked the town, haughtily exhibiting nature's supremacy over man.

"Those mountains you see in the distance, that's the La Isleta district," said Martín, seeing my amazement. "Las Palmas has several districts. Vegueta, Mesa y López, Las Canteras, and Guanarteme are the best known. Each district has its own history and customs. Vegueta, for example, is where Christopher Columbus built his house when he stopped in the Canaries on the way to the Americas. Las Canteras is the beach district."

"And La Isleta?" I asked.

"That's a dangerous district. Not somewhere you should hang around."

Martín became silent and pensive all of a sudden. We continued walking. He was hiding something from me, but I didn't try to find out more, out of respect for our friendship. We entered the town proper. It was buzzing with life. We passed a market smelling of fresh fish, then stopped in front of an old European-style building.

"We're here," declared Martín, suddenly merry again.

The man juggled emotional states like an entertainer with their clubs. He switched from a smile to a grimace in a fraction of a second, from chagrin to enthusiasm, from laughter to tears, all with a disconcerting ease that left me speechless. Martín was an enigma I was patiently trying to pierce. A mixture of uncontainable joie de vivre and sudden, overwhelming melancholy, the man seemed deeply marked by his chaotic life, wounded to the core of his being.

We entered the building and approached the reception desk, where an old lady sat wearing a look of utter boredom. A wide smile lit up her face when she saw us. *How pleasant,* I thought. Martín greeted her warmly, then started a conversation in which I understood only a few words. But I enjoyed listening to them talk, in spite of my incomprehension. Clearly intrigued by our tale, the old lady disappeared behind the reception desk and returned a few minutes later accompanied by a man who invited us to take a seat in his office. The man listened attentively as Martín explained the situation, shooting me the occasional compassionate glance as if he understood the deeply humane value of my quest. When Martín had finished speaking, the man, visibly moved, stroked his chin for a few seconds and asked us to wait while he checked the register of births, marriages, and deaths, as well as the register of foreign nationals who had moved to the island. The excitement of finally closing in on my goal rose in me like a flooded river bursting its banks. I saw a glimmer of hope in my friend's eyes too. The wait was interminable. I paced up and down. The man reappeared, looking slightly embarrassed. I immediately understood that he hadn't found anything. He apologized and wished us good luck. We left the building glumly.

"What do we do now?" I asked Martín.

"We go eat," he said with a smile. "Then we'll ask people in the street if they've come across the little girl in the picture."

"We've got no chance."

He frowned at me and I immediately regretted my hastily uttered words.

"If we have no chance, we might as well return to the ship and call it a day. You can tell the teenage boy inside you that you weren't able to find the soldier's daughter. I don't care, it's not my problem."

He crossed the street without me.

"Martín, wait!" I cried.

He turned to face me. "What is it?"

"I apologize. I agree we should show people in the street the photograph. It's a good idea."

He walked back toward me. "We have lost a battle but we haven't lost the war," he solemnly declared, his gaze filled with a certainty that chilled my blood. "If I had given up the day the Francoists shot my father in front of me, I would be dead now, hear me?"

"Yes," I timidly replied.

"So stop crying and let's go find your German girl."

The mysterious Martín began gradually to resolve. The hurt and pain within him seemed limitless. But clearly there was no place for giving up in this gaping psychological chasm. He strengthened me tenfold and I redoubled my efforts not to lose hope.

We walked for hours that afternoon, back and forth across the town, showing everyone we met the photograph of the young girl. Some stopped to listen to our story. Others, too preoccupied with their own concerns, walked right past us. Those we spoke to all replied in the negative. Nobody had seen Catherine Schäfer.

After spending several days like this, and despite our continued hope, we flopped down on the sand at Alcaravaneras Beach, exhausted from walking, our feet covered in blisters. Alcaravaneras was an odd area, seemingly working-class but with a curious social mix, situated in the east of the town not far from the port. All sorts of people rubbed shoulders here: sailors, street peddlers, middle-class professionals, and the prostitutes who thronged the promenade day and night. We granted ourselves a few moments of repose under the sun's warm caress and soon fell into a light sleep, easy prey to that confused state where images and sounds collide in an anarchic mix.

I saw a wheat field in which my actor friend Jean was yelling orders at the drill sergeant, who was pouring with sweat. My father lay on the ground beside them, eyes closed, a stalk of wheat protruding from his mouth. Mama was nearby, weeping her heart out. Jacques was there too, standing facing me, his eyes filled with rage as he screamed, "This is all your fault! This is all your fault!" The ears of wheat quivered, swept by the gusts of a storm that rumbled overhead. That's when she appeared. Mathilde. Naked, her gaze blank, she stared at me as she walked toward my brother. She took his arm and kissed him. I turned to face the forest and glimpsed the captain, who stroked his beard while yelling, "I warned you, kid!" My chest tightened increasingly with anxiety. I gasped for air. Then came the storm. Thunder boomed. Lightning struck the field, electricity arcing over our heads. Everyone disappeared except Mathilde, who whispered: "Come back, come back, I beg you," which broke my heart. A hard rain began to fall. Mathilde wandered sadly away across the field, her long legs covered with wheat. "Mathilde! Mathilde!" I screamed, hoping she'd turn around, but everything went dark. All gone. I was lost in the limbo of my unconscious.

A small voice whispered through the dark: *"Hola, hola."* Softly first, then louder and louder until I opened my eyes, terrified like a hunted animal. A woman in her thirties stood in front of me, her eyes the color of the bright-blue sky, her long hair as golden as the ears of wheat in my dream, lifted by the warm trade winds. *"Pesadilla, pesadilla,"* she said.

Martín suddenly awoke, squinting against the sunlight. He rubbed his eyes. *"Pesadilla* means 'nightmare.'" He then began a conversation with the woman, translating as he went.

"What do you want?" Martín asked her.

"Your friend was having a nightmare," she answered with a smile.

"Yes, so? It happens!"

"Sure. When one's mind is preoccupied."

"What exactly are you after?"

Offended, the woman's smile turned into a scowl.

"Nothing," she replied, walking away along the beach.

"Fucking junkies!" declared Martín, stretching back out on the sand.

It's strange, thinking back on it, but if I had not spent years cultivating my intuition—which, if I may say so, is my strongest quality—nothing that followed would ever have taken place. The woman would have gone on her way. I would have lain back down on the sand like my friend. End of story. Yet, convinced that something strange was going on, I yelled "Señora!" (one of the few Spanish words I knew) in the direction of the woman, who was already a little ways off. She turned around immediately and stood watching us with the indifference of one whose wounded pride doesn't leave them inclined to make any further effort. I roused Martín and we walked toward the woman, who stood motionless on the sand.

"Wait, madam," I said in French while Martín translated. "Sorry for having offended you. We're tired from walking around in the sun all day long. Please excuse us."

She seemed to soften, hard feelings apparently not part of her character. "Apology accepted."

"What did you want to tell us?" I was impatient to know more.

"Are you the ones searching for the German girl?"

At that, Martín and I looked at each other, amazed to be looking at the face of somebody who could help us. We might not have admitted it, but we had started to lose hope of finding Catherine.

"Yes, that's us!" I replied, feeling my internal fire burst to life even stronger than before. "How did you know?"

"You just asked one of my . . . colleagues, shall we say"—she pointed at a scantily clad prostitute strolling back and forth on the promenade—"if she had seen a little German girl."

"Yes, it's true," I said, my heart pounding in my chest. "Do you know her? Who . . . ?"

She cut me off. "My name is María," she said, holding out her hand. "I'm a streetwalker. I do it to raise my kid, who lives in Málaga, where I'm from, on the *Península*."

"The what?"

"The *Península*, Spain—that's what the Canarians call it."

María smiled sadly. It was as if all the melancholy of the world had gathered in her eyes, the corners of her mouth pointed desperately downward. She looked worn down and ruined by the street. Clearly, the woman wanted to confide in us before telling us about the German girl. I had enough respect to take an interest in this unfortunate being, wracked by the despair of existence.

"Why are you here?" I asked, intrigued.

"I followed a man here three years ago," she replied. "He made me beautiful promises—that he would marry me, bring over my little one, buy a house. But instead he beat me and sent me out on the street as soon as we arrived. And he still keeps an eye on me. I took advantage of his absence to speak with you."

We didn't know what to say, so we just nodded.

"I've not seen my little boy for three years. Manuel's his name." She showed us a picture of a sad little boy.

"He's very handsome," I said, moved.

"And what about the German girl?" asked Martín, who couldn't wait any longer.

"Show me the photograph."

I handed the picture of Catherine to María, who examined it and then gave it back to me.

"That's her, all right. Yes, I recognize her."

"Where can we find her?" Martín was quivering with impatience.

"Her mother was with us a little while ago . . . I mean, she walked the street with us."

"She walked the street?" I asked, amazed.

"Yes. Her Spanish wasn't up to much, but she was a good woman. She told us she had fled the war in Germany. She came to Gran Canaria to forget the death of her husband. She had some friends here but they didn't help her. She ran out of money. So she began to sell herself to feed her little girl."

"Did you ever see Catherine?" I asked.

"Yes, once or twice. Her mother used to take her to the beach when she wasn't working. That's where I saw her. A lovely little child, just like my Manuel . . ."

A tear rolled down her suntanned cheek. She sniffed and wiped her nose with a handkerchief.

"Where can we find her, please?"

"I don't know. They disappeared a few months ago. Since then we've not had any news. I believe they lived in a small building in La Isleta, up in the mountains over there, but I don't know where exactly."

"And you have no idea where they are now?"

"No. Her mother wanted to go somewhere else. But I have no idea where . . ."

"Is there nobody in La Isleta who could help us?" I asked.

"She was a discreet woman who focused on looking after her daughter, I don't think she had many friends there."

María lowered her gaze, aggrieved at not being able to help us further. We stayed silent for a few seconds, imagining Catherine and her mother taking flight from this place, their desperate circumstances. Chance had dealt this family a terrible hand. Catherine's father, who had gone to war to avenge his own father, had succumbed to the injuries inflicted on him by the inhabitants of my village, placing his wife and daughter at the mercy of life's vicissitudes. I had witnessed his death, powerless to intervene. A kind of guilt began to resonate in my head. After all, was I not partly responsible for this tragedy? Where did the borders of responsibility lie?

Catherine's mother had left no trace, no sign, no clue whatsoever that could point us in any direction. Where were they now? Were they still alive? I had nothing to cling to. For a moment I thought of giving up on the whole business, this unbelievable folly that had taken me to two foreign countries. What mysterious need was I trying to satisfy with my quest for truth? Mathilde was far away, alone in our empty house. I didn't even know if my letter, posted when we moored in Las Palmas, had reached her yet. Truth be told, I was weary of all the existential questionings I'd had since I was a little boy, this accumulation of nostalgia and anxiety entangled in the roots of my being. In the end, wasn't I just plain crazy, a lunatic whose whole existence was driven by a quest for recognition? Did I have a duty to suffer more than others? María earned her living, or rather lost it, by selling her body; what could be more dramatic than that? Martín had seen his father shot by the soldiers of fascism. *Life has treated me pretty well,* I thought, *and I can't hold that against it.* The *Volcan de Timanfaya* would weigh anchor that evening. We had just a few hours left to savor these last moments of tranquility. Then it would be back to the sea and its capricious swell.

22

We thanked María and bade her farewell, and she wished us safe travels. We watched her return to her place on the sidewalk next to her colleague, looking sad and lost, no doubt thinking of her little boy. I imagined little Manuel deprived of his mother, sitting on a swing, feet dangling, dejected. Can there be anything more painful than the sudden disappearance of one's mother, or one's child—the two of them inextricably linked? I thought of my mother dancing in a whirl of bubbles in the dilapidated washhouse. Why did little Manuel have to miss out on the pleasure of watching his mother intoxicated by life? I stopped dead in my tracks. Martín continued walking, not realizing I was no longer following him.

"Martín!" I called out.

He stopped and turned around.

"What is it?" he asked, looking puzzled.

"We can't let María do that . . ."

"Let her do what?"

"We can't leave her like that, she'll die here," I declared, thinking of her son.

Martín's expression turned to one of concern, as if he'd glimpsed the outline of my hastily conceived plan through a narrow keyhole. He walked toward me with a menacing air.

"We can do nothing for her, Paul. Nothing, you hear me?"

"What about her kid in Málaga, have you thought about that?"

"No, and I'd prefer not to! This doesn't concern you, my friend, you can't solve everyone's problems. That's just the way it goes. Life is unfair; it's unfair for me, it's unfair for you, for María, for everyone! So the best thing you can do now is walk with me to that damn ship and think about your wife waiting for you in Bordeaux!"

"I can't," I declared.

"Yes, you can, Paul!" Martín yelled, beside himself. "It's over, buddy. You did your best to find that German girl, you did all you could, and you should be proud of yourself! But that's the end of it."

"You told me the opposite just a few days ago. You told me that nothing's ever over."

"I said that to encourage you, Paul, nothing more. Please, trust me, there's nothing good in it for us if we go back there."

"I can't just leave her," I announced, more determined than ever.

Martín looked at me sternly. His eyes bored into mine. We remained like that, motionless, staring each other out. Passersby shot us furtive glances before continuing briskly on their way, anticipating a scuffle they wished to avoid. Eventually, Martín realized that I wouldn't back down, and his features softened. The tussle between emotion and reason had turned in my favor. He rubbed his head and sighed deeply.

"OK, what's your plan?" he asked, resigned.

"Bring María back to France with us," I said with a smile.

"How?"

"On the ship."

Martín couldn't believe his ears. He was speechless, not knowing what argument to use to make me see sense. But no words could have changed my mind.

"You're completely crazy," he said in despair.

"I know."

"The captain will never let you bring a prostitute on board."

132

"We don't have to tell him," I replied, unperturbed.

"No? What will you say when you walk up the gangway with her, Mr. Know-It-All?"

"I don't know. I'll improvise."

"You're really going to do this?"

"Yes. I can't leave her here. She didn't have to help me, but she did. Without her we'd still be out looking for Catherine. I owe her something."

"You don't owe her anything."

"Yes, I do. I must help her see her little one again."

"You've completely lost your mind."

I smiled. "Yes, I know."

I turned around and set off back along the beach. Martín begged me to be reasonable, to give up on this insane idea. I glided along, my heart pounding in my chest, thrilled to be going to the aid of a soul in distress. My body seemed in the grip of a mysterious force. In spite of his efforts, Martín understood that he could do nothing to make me turn back. "Oh, to hell with it," I heard him mutter as he followed me with a determined stride. *It's strange how manipulable men are,* I thought, as if one individual's certitude and perseverance could sweep away other people's skepticism, flooding them with one's energy, annihilating their doubts.

We soon reached the beach and saw María in the distance talking with a man. She looked desperate. We walked down to the water, taking care not to be seen by the man, who seemed excited at the idea of exploring this Andalusian's naked body, this mother who strove not to think of her son while clients shamelessly penetrated her. We watched the pair cross the street and disappear into a dimly lit building.

"What shall we do?" said Martín.

"Improvise," I replied, impatient to go help María.

We ran toward the building, adrenaline pulsing through our veins. I hoped that the man wouldn't put up any resistance, that we could appeal to his humanity. I wondered what would happen if things went awry. *Mathilde. Mama.* I would never see them again. We entered the lobby of the building. María and the man were locked in discussion with the madam, an old lady with middle-class airs, grown rich on other women's misfortune. Surprised, they turned to look at us.

"Police! Nobody move!" yelled Martín in Spanish, with a flash of inspiration.

The man's composure disappeared, swept away by the shame of being unmasked. His vices were now revealed for all to see before this figure of authority, who was anything but. He put his hands in the air and fell to his knees like a little boy confessing to his parents.

"Sorry, I didn't want to," implored the man.

"Out of the way," yelled Martín, channeling his character.

"Show me your badge!" cried the old lady, who stood her ground, used to police raids.

"One moment," stammered Martín, making as if to rummage through his pockets. "Paul, take the whore away!"

"Yes, boss!"

I grabbed María roughly by her arm. "You, come with me!" I said with authority.

María did as she was told, putting up no resistance as I pulled her out of the building. Martín finished rummaging in his pockets and produced a piece of paper, which he handed to the suspicious old lady.

"Here's my card, madam! Compliments of the Las Palmas police," he cried before exiting after me.

We ran through the town as fast as we could, crossing streets without looking, eager to reach the ship as quickly as possible, galvanized by the fear of being caught. The wind of freedom was at our backs. We finally reached the port and hid behind a pile of fishing nets, doubled up, panting. It took us a few minutes to recover. María seemed amazed at our audacity, though unaware of what was in store for her.

"What do we do now?" Martín asked once his pulse had returned to normal.

"We take her on board. She'll come back with us," I told him in French, which Martín then translated.

María stared at me wide-eyed with a mixture of fear and excitement. Then she threw herself into my arms and burst into tears. Her warm body, defiled by so many men, slumped against mine, her raspy breath on my neck. She whispered a *"Muchas gracias"* that warmed my heart. Gratitude is a delicious thing, and my soul craved it to soothe the gaping wounds of my childhood.

Now I just had to get her aboard ship, or all our efforts would be in vain and María would be left to face an uncertain future. The second stage of our improvised plan began. We approached the *Volcan de Timanfaya*. Crewmembers climbed aboard in silence one after another, in a hurry to set sail and see their families again. I glimpsed the captain at the top of the gangway, a pipe in his mouth, counting his troops with military precision. He too was in a hurry to return to the open sea. There was no way to get on board without passing in front of him. My sketchy, utopian plan came to a halt before this harsh reality. We waited a little bit in the shadow of the hull, out of the captain's line of vision. I racked my brains for a solution. The captain was waiting patiently for the entire crew to come aboard before he could weigh anchor.

"We've had it," declared Martín. "There's no solution, we'll have to leave her here."

"I'll go speak with the captain," I declared, sure of myself.

"You'll lose your job, Paul. Becoming a sailor was your dream, wasn't it?"

"If I don't bring her back, I'll stay here with her," I replied, ignoring him.

"And Mathilde?" asked Martín.

"She'll understand. I'll manage. Wait for me here."

"Hurry up. The ship will be leaving soon!"

I walked to the bottom of the gangway, stopped, and looked up. The captain watched me, drawing on his pipe and expelling great clouds of smoke that wafted away on the breeze. I gestured at him to come down. He didn't understand, so I repeated the gesture. He descended the gangway.

"What's up, Vertune?" he asked, removing the pipe from his mouth.

"Captain, you're going to kill me."

He scowled. "Why?"

"Do you recall how you told me that life isn't always easy, that we can't always do what we want?"

"Yes."

"I got the message."

"Meaning?"

"That woman you see over there beside Martín helped me pick up the trail of the family of a soldier who spared my life during the war. When he died, I found a picture of his daughter on him, and I swore I'd find her."

"And did you?" he asked, intrigued by my story.

"No. The trail went cold."

"What's the connection with her?" He nodded in María's direction.

"She met the woman while working the streets of Las Palmas."

"You mean she's a prostitute?"

"Yes, Captain. She was forced into it. She hasn't seen her little boy for three years. He's back in Spain."

"And what's that to do with me?"

"I want to take her with us, Captain."

"Have you lost your mind, Vertune? We'll be taking no passengers on this ship! Leave her here on the quay and get on board, we weigh anchor in ten minutes," he said coldly, turning to ascend the gangway.

"Captain, I beg you. If she doesn't come with us, I'm staying here."

He stopped dead in his tracks, took a long draw on his pipe, then turned to face me.

"Are you threatening me, Vertune?" he asked sternly.

"No, Captain. But I'm begging you to help her."

He drew on his pipe again, exhaled another stream of smoke, looked at Martín and María for a few moments, then stared hard at me.

"You have faith in humanity, don't you, Vertune?"

"Yes, Captain."

"You're young and idealistic." He sniggered and contemplated the glowing embers of his pipe. "I used to be like you, full of hope and illusions regarding human nature." He sniggered again.

Suddenly he scowled.

"Then I lowered my guard one day. Three guys attacked me and beat me until I could no longer stand. I nearly died on the quayside. All for a fistful of cash."

He stroked the stem of his pipe, took another draw, and looked me straight in the eye.

"Man is cruel, Vertune, and life's a bitch who eats her young when she's starving. She never does us any favors, she's not generous. The sooner you understand that the better, or you'll end up like me. I don't like life, Vertune, and life doesn't like me."

"Exactly, Captain, I'm giving you the opportunity to make your peace with it!" I exclaimed.

He removed his pipe from his mouth and frowned. "Make my peace with it?"

"Yes, Captain, make your peace with life by reawakening the young man inside of you."

The man froze and his expression darkened. For a moment I regretted my hastily uttered words. He seemed to be staring straight through me, lost in some distant childhood memory. His pipe had gone out, and a delicate odor of damp tobacco floated in the air.

"Become a young man again, you say?"

"Yes, Captain. Because a young man believes in humanity. He has yet to endure tragedy, the hard blows of fate, mankind's cruelty. This prostitute's little boy is somewhere in Andalusia, alone, crying every day for his mother. If you help María get out of here, Captain, you'll be doing all humanity a service, believe me, and that feeling is worth more than all the mistresses in the world."

He stared at me, obviously dumbfounded by the sincerity of my words and my soul's strength of character. A moment passed. Then he struck a match, relit the embers of his pipe, and took a long draw.

"You're completely crazy, Vertune. But I like that. It's as if I'm looking at myself thirty years ago. Bring her up and put her in cabin 308. It's empty. I don't want her to leave it for a single second during the whole crossing, do you understand me?"

"Yes, Captain."

"Very good, we'll weigh anchor."

"Captain?"

"What now, Vertune?"

"Thank you."

23

We berthed in Bordeaux two weeks later in the midst of a light drizzle. The contrast with the Canary Islands was striking. No sun here, no ocean, no bright-blue sky. In just a few days we had sailed between two parallel worlds, two geographical locations so close and yet so different. *That's the magic of the sea,* I thought, *and of the sailor's profession too.*

The crossing had not presented any difficulties. The ocean waves had let us off lightly this time. María remained shut up in her cabin, meditative, in a hurry to reach terra firma and see her little Manuel again. I visited her cabin once a day and brought meals, which she wolfed down, taking advantage of my presence to speak to me a little. I didn't understand much at first, but over the course of the voyage I learned enough Spanish to grasp the gist of her words. A spark of gratitude shone in her eyes. *"Muchas gracias, Paul, usted es un santo, "* she said every time I opened the door to her cabin, making sure nobody had seen me. I was thus a "saint," canonized by the beautiful María, who, for the first time in a long while, didn't have to fear being raped. In the close quarters of her ocean prison, María had regained her taste for life.

A few sailors had seen María come aboard ship the day of our departure. The rumor of a woman on board had fueled the conversations and fantasies of these men deprived of female company. But they quieted down the day the captain raised his voice and explained that María was just a charwoman whom he had brought on board to clean his cabin. One more lie wouldn't kill the old man, and marital infidelities were so common in this itinerant business that they interested no one. To my great relief, the crew returned to their (more professional) occupations. As for Martín, he asked me for news of our mutual friend from time to time, proud to have played a part in freeing her, despite his initial reticence. His flash of inspiration at the short-stay hotel had bought us time without having to resort to violence. I had congratulated him, but he'd simply shrugged as if it was an obvious thing to do, with such false modesty it had made me smile. In truth, he was overjoyed at being complimented for his actions.

On the quayside in Bordeaux stood a group of women eager to see their husbands again. They waved their arms in the air to greet us, their heroes of the sea. I tried to make out the figure of my wife in the crowd, without success. Mathilde had no doubt been kept back by Madame de Saint-Maixent. The sailors disembarked one after another, impatient to see their families again. Martín and I waited until there was no one left on board before rushing down the passageways to María's cabin. I opened the door and we found her curled up on the floor, tears running down her cheeks. Martín crouched beside her and gave her a sad smile.

"María, it's time to leave," he said softly.

"I don't know where to go. I'm scared."

"You'll come to my place, and tomorrow we'll put you on a train to Málaga so you can see Manuel."

"What if he doesn't recognize me? What if he doesn't know who I am? I want to go back to Las Palmas. Leave me on board, I don't want to get off."

Martín stood up without a word and stroked his stubbly beard, barely stiffer than a teenager's fluff. He didn't know how to reply. María seemed overwhelmed, beset by her imagination, which had sown seeds of doubt regarding this adventure. She hugged her knees to her chest and gently rocked to and fro on the cold floor. Poor María, cast out on the street, had never lost hope of seeing her child again one day. She yearned for him with all her being, with every fiber of her body, willing to die just to hold him again. But now that the goal was in sight, she couldn't, just couldn't keep going. What strange mechanism had filled this woman with the sudden fear of not being worthy of her son?

"María, get up," I said softly. "Don't worry about your little one, he'll recognize you. A child never forgets their mother's scent, believe me."

María stopped her rocking and looked at me.

"Are you sure?" she whispered.

"Quite sure," I replied.

"I believe you, Paul. You're a good man, you know."

"Thank you María. Get up now, we have to go."

I helped her to her feet. We made our way through the maze of passageways, which I now knew by heart. When we reached the open air, María took a deep breath, closing her eyes as she did so. *"¡Qué bueno!"* she murmured. The three of us descended the gangway and stepped onto dry land. I scanned the quayside for Mathilde, but there was no one around. Maybe she had forgotten the precise time of our arrival. I wasn't worried, though I couldn't wait to see her and kiss her. But first I had to say goodbye to María.

"This is where we go our separate ways," I said.

"Muchas gracias, Paul. I'll never forget what you've done for me. One day I'll return the favor."

She kissed my cheek. The touch of her soft, warm lips made me shiver.

"Take care of yourself, María, and give your son a kiss from me. Here is my address, please send me some pictures of him." I handed her an envelope, which she put in her pocket.

"I certainly will. God bless you, Paul Vertune."

Her face shone with the gratitude of a woman saved from a life of sexual violence. She turned to Martín and they walked toward his house, located not far from the port. At the corner, María turned to wave and mouth a final *"Gracias"* before they disappeared from view.

The heavy weight of responsibility slipped from me and shattered on the cobblestones of the quayside. I felt at peace, in harmony with myself. What a lovely sensation it was. No more worrying, no more fears, just the feeling of having accomplished what I said I'd do, the satisfaction of having helped María.

But there was something else.

The previous evening, as I slipped my address into the envelope for María, I'd had a sudden urge to be done with this Catherine Schäfer business. I had taken senseless risks to find her, putting my life in peril in Germany and Spain without considering the consequences, all for this enigmatic quest that had obsessed me for years. I wanted to forget about this whole business and focus on Mathilde. I missed my wife enormously. We had plenty of living to do as a couple. So when I prepared the envelope for María, I also put the picture of Catherine Schäfer in it, a kind of souvenir of our meeting. I had to hold back my tears as the little girl's image disappeared into the envelope. A chapter of my story had drawn to a close. It was time to return home. *End of my first voyage,* I thought, hoping that not all my future ones would be quite so dramatic.

I had turned to look back at the ship when I saw her, standing in the rain, her wet hair plastered to her face. Her clothes were soaked through, the drizzle having been followed by a sudden rainstorm. She looked stunning, my Mathilde, even in her sodden outfit, a mix of the sun and the moon and the stars. Her long dress hugged her slender figure perfectly. I walked over and took her in my arms. She was freezing.

"I love you, Mathilde."

"I love you too, Paul."

"You're frozen, let's get home quick."

"Wait. I've got something to tell you."

"What?"

"I'm pregnant."

Day and night were as one, earth and ocean entangled in absolute silence. And then it was all a blur. This announcement of fatherhood plucked me from my surroundings like one plucks summer daisies to make a crown. I instinctively thought of my father with the ever-present stalk of wheat in his mouth. Now I would come to know the great thrill of birth and a child's love for their parents. Life is a piece of theater that every generation makes its own by playing the characters differently, giving them fresh depth and improving the rhythm of the performance. Sometimes the audience rises to its feet and applauds, won over by the changes made. Sometimes it stays seated, bored, preferring the original to the new version. I was already imagining a splendid theater piece in which the character to be born would play a major role. Was I prepared for fatherhood? I hugged my wife tightly, imagining the fruit of our love in her belly. Now we were three.

24

"Push it out, quick!" exclaimed the nervous midwife.

"Aaaaah!" Mathilde screamed in pain.

"It's nearly over, just one more push, come on, harder!"

"Aaaaah!"

When the head of my child emerged from between my wife's thighs, I initially thought I would pass out. With a mixture of admiration and disgust before nature at work, I understood why my father had claimed he had an urgent task the day of my birth. Blood gushed from my wife's vagina, covering the face of the child whose gender I could not yet discern. The midwife grabbed the newborn, cut the umbilical cord, and wrapped the baby in a white towel that immediately began to stain red.

"It's a girl," she declared, smiling. "Congratulations!"

"Thank you," I replied, unsettled by the announcement.

"What's her name?"

"I . . . I . . ." I stammered, spooked by the blood and the baby's cries.

"Jeanne!" cried Mathilde. "Her name is Jeanne."

I felt strange, very strange. Mathilde's pregnancy had passed without complications. Her belly had swelled as I went back and forth to sea. I was assailed by guilt as Mathilde confronted the trial that is pregnancy, that storm of hormones. But I had no choice; we had to eat. Mathilde stopped working for the last two months, disrupting the routine of Madame de Saint-Maixent, who stopped paying her salary, upset at being abandoned. The benevolence of the bourgeoisie had its limits—in this case, those of Madame's unhealthy self-centeredness and her inability to conceive of happiness in any other household. Misery is the surest fuel of jealousy.

The midwife wiped Jeanne's frail little body, removing the blood from her limbs and face. Then she placed the crying baby on a set of scales, examined her with a stethoscope, and inflicted the full battery of traditional tests to check that she was in good health. When she had completed her barbaric but necessary ritual, she swaddled Jeanne in a fresh towel and handed the infant to her mother. Mathilde tenderly cradled her and she slowly quieted down. The midwife helped her pull a breast free for the newborn to suckle. Silence filled the room once more. I leaned in and contemplated my daughter's face. Everything about her was tiny and delicate: her hands, her feet, her skin, her nose, her mouth stuck to Mathilde's nipple. And still so untouched by life's vicissitudes. This was the start of the race to death, the inexorable countdown to the end that nobody can escape but everyone attempts to forget in their own way. My daughter would not escape either. Until that moment, the notion that she might suffer in this world had not even crossed my mind.

"She's beautiful," I murmured to Mathilde, caressing the infant's cheek.

"Yes."

"She's the spitting image of you. She has your eyes."

Mathilde smiled shyly. We took our daughter home the next day and settled her in the crib that a generous neighbor had given us. It was far from the opulence of Madame de Saint-Maixent's house, but our living conditions were a distinct improvement over those I had known as a child. My daughter had the privacy of her own room. Not that I was jealous, quite the opposite; to each their own era and set of troubles—but as few as possible for Jeanne, I hoped with all my heart.

◆ ◆ ◆

145

Unlike her rural parents, Jeanne grew up in a buzzing, booming city, its busy port a confluence of distant civilizations. Mathilde went back to work for Madame de Saint-Maixent, who rehired her the day our daughter was old enough to attend nursery school. As for me, I was promoted to a ship plying the Europe–Asia route. This took me to sea for long periods, often more than four months at a time. Whenever I embarked, the two women in my life waved me goodbye from the quayside. They cried their eyes out. They were inconsolable. It filled me with sorrow, but it was the price I had to pay to keep my dream alive. When the ship docked back in Bordeaux several months later, I was sad to see how much Jeanne had grown in my absence.

The shipping company now gave me two months' home leave each year so I could make the most of my family before returning to the tempestuous ocean. Each summer, we vacationed in Brittany with our families. I was enchanted with the idea of Jeanne discovering the place in which her mother and I had grown up. She spent many happy days on the beaches of our childhood, laughing as she gathered shells covered in silt, stopping to stare, astonished, at a crab scuttling over the pebbles. Sometimes, hiding behind a tree in the garden of the Vertune farmhouse, I watched my daughter marveling at the simple pleasures of life. She would pick up a fallen apple, bring it close to her eyes, and attempt to pierce the mystery of this fruit, using her little girl's pure imagination. And thus I too became a child again behind my apple tree, moved when I saw in her certain characteristics of my own personality.

Fatherhood offers a chance to rediscover one's past, to ward off an unhappy childhood or prolong the pleasure of a golden one. It is not something you pick up in a drugstore to dress your wounds. On the contrary, it gives you the opportunity to rejuvenate, as long as you don't overdo it. I leapt at the opportunity to become a child once more, playing with Jeanne for hours, imitating wild animals. Jeanne giggled wildly when I played a gorilla thumping his chest, a seal flopping about on the icy floor of its blue islet, or a rhinoceros charging between the apple trees. Finally, tired of playing in the sun, we lay on the grass, her little body snuggled up to mine.

"Why is the sky blue, Papa?" she asked, curious like her father.

"Because it wanted to be friends with the sea," I spontaneously replied.

"Why did it want to be friends with the sea?"

"Because the sea is kind."

"Is the sea kind to you, Papa?"

"Yes, except when there's a gale."

"What's a gale?"

"Wind, Jeanne, lots of wind."

When she was satisfied with my answers, she began to daydream, sometimes falling asleep in the shadow of the trees. I would gather her in my arms and carry her to bed, where she'd continue her siesta.

We visited my brothers, who were also married to local girls, as tradition required. Pierre and Guy lived not far from the Vertune farm, still helping my eldest brother in the wheat fields. Technical progress and the appearance of combine harvesters had made the work and their lives much easier. Ever true to themselves, they spoke little and acquiesced without argument, fleeing conflict like the plague. Jacques, as unrelenting as ever in his work, had softened with age, however. He was father to an adorable little boy on whom he doted, attentive to his slightest wish, talking and listening to him in a way we had never known as children. Our relationship improved over time, even if it never reached my hoped-for heights, that brotherly solidarity we had briefly known in the back of the Germans' truck the day I first saw Mathilde.

When I was a child, brotherly relations had seemed like sanctuaries from which each of us drew strength, like a well from which one carefully collects water, making sure never to let it run dry. Any argument or conflict between brothers was simply unthinkable. I thought that my brothers would always be at my side, that they would stand by me through life's ups and downs, heartaches, betrayals. But, idealistic as I was, I quickly lost those illusions as I noticed how my brothers became more withdrawn in front of my father, contrasting with our carefree behavior as we scampered about the woods and trails. I grew disheartened the more abuse I received, prompting my departure from the family cocoon to make my own way. Even if they were all proud of having a sailor brother, nothing would ever be like before. Still, we happily passed the time digging for clams, picnicking on the beach, and teaching the kids to skim stones across the water.

Mathilde's father was around too. He watched his daughter and his granddaughter with loving eyes. What wouldn't he have given to still have his wife by his side?

Finally, in late August, this pleasant parenthesis would always come to an end, as the three of us packed up and returned to Bordeaux. Jeanne shyly waved goodbye to her grandparents through the train window. Mama shed a few tears as we pulled out of the station, bereft of a child she'd have preferred to keep close.

"Granny gone!" said Jeanne, still too young to understand what was happening.

"Yes, gone!" I repeated to my daughter. "We'll see her next year, OK?"

"Granny always gone. Like you, Papa!"

Children may only be children, but they are clever nonetheless. And Jeanne was tremendously clever. She was beginning to understand that her father deserted her, that he was obliged to leave on his ship "for work." But what does the word *work* mean to kids? *Not much,* I thought. I was reaching the limits of my childhood dream. As much as I loved my job, I felt guiltier every passing day at not being around more for my daughter. The captain of my first ship, recently retired, had warned me: "A sailor's life is a tough one, you don't get to watch your children grow up." The old sea dog was right. I could already anticipate my daughter's reproaches about my cyclical absences. I had suffered my father's lack of communication; now my daughter was suffering my abandonment, which imperiled our future relationship. But I didn't want to have to make a choice. Selfishly, I wanted to prolong my freedom for as long as possible.

I embarked again each September, not to return until January. Now that I was working the intercontinental shipping routes, I came into contact with all kinds of people and cultures. It seemed to me that, physical appearance aside, humanity was a single, indivisible whole. Only the languages changed. I saw the same smiles in West Africa, Asia, and Oceania. The warm welcome extended us by native populations warmed our hearts after long months spent at sea. On our few days of shore leave, Martín and I would head off into the hinterlands to meet the locals and discover their customs and habits. I felt as if I were in some way perfecting my education in the field by combining theory and practice. Monsieur Duquerre, my old schoolmaster, would have been proud.

I received news from María on several occasions. Every year she sent me a postcard on which she scribbled a few sentences in Spanish, which Martín helped me understand. She also slipped a picture of her son into the envelope, so I saw him grow up as the years passed. She never mentioned the picture of Catherine Schäfer. But after ten years or so, she stopped writing. What I initially thought was an oversight ended up worrying me. I decided to write to her to make sure that everything was fine. The envelope was returned a few weeks later marked *Addressee Unknown*. I re-sent the letter several times, thinking the postal service had messed up. Mistakes happen, after all. But each time, the envelope was returned in the same manner. Martín called the Málaga town hall, but they were unable to help us. The secretary on the other end of the line assured us she would make further inquiries, but we heard nothing more from her. María had disappeared without a trace. Worried at her sudden disappearance, I called her local police station several times. We even got hold of a neighbor's telephone number, but it was always the same: nobody knew where María was.

What lay behind this mysterious disappearance? I was frustrated at not being able to investigate properly, since I spent most of my home leave making up for lost time with Jeanne. Mathilde sensed my growing concern and tried to reassure me, but her efforts were in vain. In spite of my religious skepticism, I secretly prayed that nothing had happened to María. For a long time, whenever the doorbell rang, I would walk down the corridor hoping I'd open the door to find María there with her son, Manuel. I would take a deep breath before turning the doorknob, but each time brought the same disappointment. The years passed and I came to terms with it. One soon learns to forget. Besides, María owed me nothing. I had helped her out of the goodness of my heart, out of human kindness, not for her to spend her whole life thanking me in return. I was nobody's hero. I was just a man. Why try to change the world when you are incapable of changing yourself?

With María's disappearance went many of my illusions. We all grow up one day or another. At our own pace. Thanks to her, I grew up too, the day I understood that the world wasn't made in my image, but rather that it was up to me to adapt myself to the world.

25

July 17, 1965. A series of letters and numbers. An unexceptional date, devoid of significance, at least to most of humanity. Our days pass like shooting stars in the sky. We pause to watch them for a moment, fascinated by the strangeness of their origins. When they start to fade, when the show is no longer entertaining enough, we return to our everyday business, already bored with their enchanting trails. But July 17, 1965, is of indelible importance to me.

Three weeks before, we had rounded the Cape of Good Hope. A thick fog masked the South African coast beneath its white veil. I imagined I could make out gates to the Indian Ocean standing majestically in the ship's path, their hinges invisible to the naked eye. As we drew near, these imaginary gates opened with an ear-piercing creak, like chalk screeching across a blackboard. The gates bore a coat of arms depicting Poseidon with his thick, wild beard (similar to those of my schoolmaster and my first captain) brandishing his trident aloft to prove his supremacy. He smiled a mischievous smile through the drifting fog, as if wishing us good fortune, or perhaps warning us of impending danger. Once we had passed, the gates closed with the same din and were soon shrouded from view.

We were now sailing toward beautiful Saigon, our final destination. The weather seemed relatively clement, despite the incessant rain. The sailors slipped about on the wet deck, cursing fiercely and clutching their bruised limbs.

Entering the Indian Ocean was serious business, subject to a slew of safety measures and procedures to adopt in the event of an emergency. At this point of latitude—the Roaring Forties—ships run the gauntlet of the most powerful winds on earth and the most destructive waves, where even large vessels may be broken into matchwood by the force of the swell. A moment's inattention in these waters can come at a heavy price. All the sailors knew the risks. No place for lack of discipline, or for anything less than precision. Maritime regulations were respected to the letter and excessively checked and rechecked by the captain. The whole crew worked together as one, making sure the cargo was properly lashed down, the engines running smoothly, and the pumps prepped.

As the African coast receded, I sensed a growing, palpable tension in each of us, like that felt by parents removing the training wheels from their child's bike. The company's executives, ensconced in their plush leather armchairs on the other side of the globe, maintained a constant pressure on the captain over the radio, interrogating him about the state of the cargo and urging him to reach port as fast as he could. Amid this flow of instructions, there was no concern at all for the welfare of the crew. That the ship was keeping to schedule mattered far more to them than the human beings responsible for ensuring delivery of the cargo. We were mere cogs in their profit-generating apparatus. But despite the risks, I loved the ocean all the same, that blue expanse full of mystery and danger, which forced individuals to stick together, demonstrating a solidarity they would never have shown in other circumstances.

◆ ◆ ◆

We had been moving through the rough waters of the Indian Ocean for three weeks and couldn't wait to sight land again. Some sailors, frustrated by the long crossing and the absence of women, spoke openly of visiting prostitutes once we reached Saigon. There was a kind of vanity in their words, as if those poor women were hunting trophies to be hung on the wall. I was stirred from my reveries by the sound of the ship's siren summoning us all on deck. Martín, with whom I'd been sharing a cabin for a decade now, put down the book he'd had his nose stuck in and peeked at the sea through the porthole.

"Looks calm," he said vacantly.

"And the clouds?" I asked with the expert interest of a young sea dog.

"There aren't any. It's nearly dusk."

"Everything's fine, then. It's just a drill."

"I'm not so sure," replied Martín skeptically.

"How's that?"

"I've got a bad feeling."

"Are you psychic now?" I joked.

"I sense that something's going to happen. Get your gear on and let's head up top."

I didn't reply. Martín had spoken with none of his usual verve, he who usually accompanied every phrase with much gesticulation. He stood by the porthole, looking serious. He seemed preoccupied. I didn't want to press him further. We pulled on our gear and made our way through the maze of passages.

Chaos reigned. People were running in all directions. The access stairways to the upper decks were congested. I asked a few random sailors what was going on, but none were any the wiser. *Strange,* I thought. We climbed one set of stairs after another, finally emerging onto the open deck. It was like stepping into an oven, the air unbearably thick and heavy. Martín still seemed just as preoccupied. *What could be on his mind?* Suddenly we heard cries from the other side of the ship. Moving as one, we rushed aft, then crossed the rear deck. There, on the starboard deck, stood a group of sailors pointing at the horizon in awe and wonder. I followed their gaze and what I saw remains forever etched in my memory.

In the dying light, I witnessed a spectacle of breathtaking, uninhibited nature. A pale quarter moon shone high in the sky, its bluish-white light reflected on the water, decorating the sea with thousands of shimmering creases. Grandiose, I tell you. But all attention was focused not on the moon but on the horizon, where vast clouds amassed toward the stars. They seemed almost to be draining the ocean of its energy and force. What I found most strange was the surprising demarcation between darkness and light, just above the horizon, as if nature were imposing upon us a frontier we little beings shouldn't breach, no matter how used we were to flouting nature's laws. The warning seemed clear: cross this border and we would be at the mercy of this chaos, of the elements unchained, in peril of our lives.

Long streaks of lightning ripped through the sky, licking at the sea. The rumbling thunder reached us a few seconds later, like the beating of a tautly stretched drum announcing an imminent execution. *What extravagance,* I told myself, *what beauty amid chaos, what surreal decor.* This was why I had become a sailor, to escape humdrum everyday life and experience such moments of intense excitement. It was too late to turn and run. The storm was simply too near, and closing fast. Our ship was on an inescapable course to either catastrophe or glory. I shuddered.

"We're going to die!" exclaimed a young sailor.

"No, we're not, it's just a storm," declared another.

"May God have pity on us."

"Stop your blabbing, you bunch of milksops!"

The captain shoved his way through the gathered sailors, castigating his men left and right. When he reached the guardrail and got a clear view, he paused, momentarily dumbfounded.

"That's a cyclone," he stated calmly, though he was clearly also terrified.

"A cyclone, Captain?"

"Yes. They announced one far from here on the radio a few days ago. They got it wrong. Those morons at the company. I hate them."

"What do we do, Captain?" I asked.

"We pray."

Then he turned to the amassed sailors contemplating the horizon.

"Gentlemen, this is the moment you've been waiting for, ever since you became sailors," he yelled, finger pointing at the sky. "May I present a cyclone. It is rare to meet one at sea, for usually we are warned of this kind of thing over the radio, but since our company is staffed by assholes, we shall have to ride it out! Gentlemen, know that this is an honor bestowed on us by nature, so let us ensure we are worthy of it!"

A few shouts of joy were soon drowned out by the crew's skeptical mumblings.

"Action stations!" screamed the captain. "I want every man at his post, but no one on deck at any point! In a few hours it'll be a war zone up here. Lock every door and access hatch. Don't even think of eating, it'll be wasted when you puke your guts out! Don't sleep, you couldn't if you tried! Don't bother taking a piss, you'll be wetting yourselves soon enough! Don't think about anything but reaching Saigon. The company will pick up the entire crew's tab at the whorehouse! And one more thing: it has been an honor to sail with you, my dear shipmates."

The captain's words didn't bode well at all. The rumble of the approaching storm grew louder, and the crew redoubled their efforts to get everything shipshape. My sweet moon still smiled in the sky, and I winked at it before disappearing into what might become my tomb, praying we'd be spared. I thought of Jeanne, the little girl I had been neglecting since she was born; Mathilde, the wife abandoned for my childhood dream; María, from whom I'd had no more news; Catherine Schäfer, now a grown woman; Jean, who was pursuing a fine career in Paris as an actor; Mama; and my brothers. I hoped with all my heart that I'd see them again.

26

The natural elements are capricious, murderous, and thoroughly unscrupulous. Sometimes, when their accumulated resentment of us humans reaches a tipping point, they band together to let us know we are merely tenants, passing through. They alone are the true landlords. That night, we on the ship paid the arrears on humanity's rent.

We felt the first effects of the rough swell against the ship's hull a few minutes after heading below deck. The rain began to fall—softly at first, then ever more violently as the minutes passed. The wind began to whistle through door cracks and porthole gaps as the booming thunder grew inexorably closer. Some sailors howled with joy at the idea of braving the cyclone. Others, scared and worried, said nothing.

The swell became more extreme. The wind shrieked through the ship. We went down into the hold to make sure the cargo wasn't being shaken about by the rough swell. It all seemed in order. We clambered back up through the passageways, grabbing hold of door handles and bulkheads to pull ourselves forward. Where was Martín? I hadn't seen him for the past few hours, which worried me. What could be bothering him? After all, it was only a storm—a bad one, for sure, but just a storm nonetheless.

The ship was now pitching and rolling much more violently. Concerned about my missing friend, I went back down the passageways to our cabin to check if Martín was there. Progress was slow as I staggered to keep my balance. Finally I reached the cabin. Martín was sitting on his bed, eyes fixed on the floor, lost in his thoughts. He seemed frozen in this position and didn't look up when I entered. I sat down beside my best friend.

"Everything all right, man?" I asked.

"I'm going to die, Paul," he calmly replied.

"Cut the bullshit, it's just a storm, nothing more."

"No. You don't understand. It's Judgment Day."

"Judgment Day?" I was both intrigued by his mysticism and scared by the confidence in his tone.

"Yes."

"What the hell do you mean? What's going on?"

"This ship reeks of death, Paul," he replied with an equanimity that made my blood run cold. "The same death I saw in my father's eyes when he crumpled before me, his chest riddled with bullets. I can smell it. It's here all around us, lying in wait."

My heart skipped a beat. A paralyzing fear seized my limbs. I was incapable of responding, of asking him where he got such a gruesome idea.

"You know, Paul," he continued in the same even tone, "you are my best friend. The day I met you I immediately knew you were different from the rest. It's what drew me to you. And then there was María. You saved her."

"*We* saved her."

"No. I didn't agree to, at first. If it wasn't for you, she'd still be walking the streets in Las Palmas."

"It was you who urged me to continue the search for news of Catherine," I replied. "Without you, I would have left empty-handed. Life is about teamwork, Martín."

"Perhaps." He shot me a smile. "Either way, she's free now."

"What are you getting at?"

Lightning flashed through the porthole, flooding the cabin with ephemeral clarity, immediately followed by the deafening crash of thunder. Chaos reigned outside.

"Nothing," replied Martín a little louder. "This is where it all ends, my friend."

"But how can you be so sure of that?"

"Carmen told me."

"Who's Carmen?"

"A girl I met many years ago."

"Where?"

"In Spain."

"I don't know what you're talking about, Martín. You're scaring me! Come up to the second deck! Right now!"

"After my father died," he continued, heedless, "my life was in chaos. I drank, went out all the time, slept with random girls. I was a mess. Nothing made sense anymore. Alcohol was my sole distraction, my sole pleasure. I forgot about everything else. And then I walked into a bar one day and I met Carmen."

Something softened in his face as he pronounced her name, and gradually my friend's personality returned, excited by the memory of this woman.

"I can still smell her jasmine perfume," he continued, sniffing the air. "We slept together for months. I frittered away all my savings just to be with her, spending hours on end in bed, our bodies intertwined. Her presence brought back my smile, my hope. She was so beautiful, my Carmen. I kept asking her to marry me. She told me she belonged to another. She never wanted to tell me who."

"I don't get it, Martín."

His smile vanished abruptly, his gaze darkened.

"I rented us a hotel room that night. We made love several times. Then she drifted off to sleep. In the half-light I softly stroked her skin, still faintly scented with jasmine. I would have given everything for her to become my wife. Suddenly, her body stiffened, like a rigid piece of wood. Her eyes rolled back in their sockets and her hands seized my throat with incredible force. In a very deep, masculine voice she yelled, over and over: 'Your soul will burn in the chaos of the ocean.' It was no longer Carmen speaking, Paul, but the devil. I managed to pull myself free and took to my heels, trembling with fear."

I was dumbstruck by his tale. I thought about trying to persuade him that it was just a dream, that demonic possession isn't real, that there was surely a rational explanation, but I thought better of it. Who was I, after all, to doubt his words and challenge his assertions? Martín was a sensitive soul who had suffered much in life.

"A few days later, I returned to the bar she frequented and asked to see her. They told me they knew of no such person . . ."

"Get a hold of yourself, Martín, I beg you, and come with me!"

"I never understood the meaning of her words. That's why I went to sea, to understand. Now here I am."

"Where?"

"Life is but an illusion," he said sadly. "An illusion where love withers and childhood dreams fade. Men are cruel, Paul, so very cruel. Only women are capable of reversing our death spiral, our inner turmoil. Carmen meant everything to me. I miss her. She alone could—"

A violent jolt interrupted him and knocked us to the floor. The ship groaned as it twisted beneath the force of the waves. Then came the warning siren. Then a crash of thunder, followed by intense flashes of lightning that seared our eyes. Another awful jolt. The ship seemed to plunge into an abyss at breakneck speed before pitching up an infinite slope, then rolling from one side to the other. We were thrown about the cabin, smashing into the beds and lockers.

"It's Judgment Day, Paul!" yelled Martín as if in a trance. "Feel his strength, his power, his . . ."

A fresh jolt, even more violent. The ship seemed to hang in the air, and I felt like we were sliding backward. We just had time to grab onto the handles of the lockers when another impact shook the steel structure. More creaking and groaning. Surely the apocalypse was nigh and shipwreck imminent? We heard cries of terror from the passageway, howls of supplication for this nightmare to end. I had an image of Mama praying in her little village church. I sat beside her and prayed in silence too, sheltered from the fury outside, asking for life to grant me another few years so I could hug and kiss my daughter and my wife, and stretch out in the shade of the orchard of my childhood one last time.

The juddering and the crashes of thunder brought back memories of the bombing raids when I was a boy. How much longer could we stand this? An hour? A day? A week? Any notion of time ceases when existence itself falters. Only the present moment counts, that moment we all usually flee, preferring to wallow in the sweet nostalgia of the past or the stimulating dread of the future. *Let me see my daughter again, I beg you.*

More groaning from the tortured metal. What was happening?

Dear God, we've never spoken much, but I swear I'll be there for my family from now on. I've learned my lesson.

A thin stream of water flowed under the cabin door. Martín, lying on the floor, didn't react. He seemed lifeless, absent. I thought about the *Titanic,* that huge ocean liner swallowed by the sea, all those people thrown into the freezing waters of the North Atlantic. *At least we have the good fortune to be sailing warmer waters,* I said to myself, by way of consolation. Soon the water was up to our knees. Its temperature was not unpleasant.

Another huge jolt. The warning siren suddenly stopped. What use was it anyway when we were all headed for certain watery death? No point fighting the apocalypse.

Lightning. Thunder. Rain. Wind. Waves. It was all a blur. It seemed as if the porthole was submerged, that the ship was diving to the deep. *My God, it's all over. We have to get out of here at all costs, right now.* I grabbed Martín and slapped him full in the face. He suddenly came to his senses and smiled.

"We can't do anything, Paul. The devil told me so."

160

I shook him as hard as I could.

"Shut up, Martín, for God's sake!"

Using all my strength, I dragged him out of the cabin. Water sloshed around us. A few yards along the passageway, two bodies were floating. We stepped over them in horror. The water around them was red from the blood seeping from their head wounds.

"This way!" came a voice from the end of the passageway.

I made out a muscular figure.

"Help us!" I shouted.

The man disappeared. Everyone was trying to save their own skin as best they could. We made our way to the end of the passageway and hauled ourselves up the wet steps. Martín slipped and I caught him.

Another jolt. I imagined Mathilde reading the newspaper to Madame de Saint-Maixent, Jeanne heading off to school, Mama scrubbing clothes in her washhouse. Could they have imagined for a single moment the situation their man was currently in?

We continued our progress with difficulty, battling the shaking and the water that seemed to be seeping in everywhere.

"Help!" I yelled without much conviction.

The passageways were empty, apart from the floating bodies of unfortunate souls who must have hit a bulkhead too hard. Where was everyone?

Nature granted us a few moments of respite from the juddering and jolting, time standing still for what seemed like hours, allowing us to make it up another stairway and onto the second deck. I recognized the muscular figure of the man in front of us.

"Help!" I yelled again in the direction of the retreating figure.

"This way," he cried, turning around. "Follow me!"

"Where are you going?"

"I . . . I . . . don't know." My question seemed to disturb him.

Another jolt. The ship rolled violently to one side. Martín lost his grip and slid to the end of the passageway while I grabbed hold of a door that opened under the pressure of my body, sending me half-sprawling into a cabin. Lightning flashed through the porthole—this part of the ship was above water—illuminating a man curled up into a ball on his bunk. He was surprised to see me.

"Get up," I shouted, "we have to get out of here!"

He looked at me questioningly.

"And go where?"

I didn't know how to answer. I hauled myself back into the passageway, leaving the man alone in his little cabin. There was no sign of the muscular guy from before. Martín too had disappeared. The bulb above me flickered. The ship's fuses held out for a few more seconds, before a final flickering, then darkness. The ship pitched violently again.

I thought for a moment. There was just one more stairway to climb, then another passageway. I knew the ship like the back of my hand. But where was Martín? I screamed his name repeatedly. The only reply was the creaking of the hull. *Find Martín or escape?* I chose my friend, without a shadow of hesitation. I retraced my steps, groping my way along the passageway, grabbing hold of doorknobs either to aid my climb or slow my descent. Water sloshed up and down, soaking me through. I screamed his name again. Still no answer. I persisted, waving my hands in front of me like a blind man without a cane. I finally reached the stairway and shouted: "Martín!"

Silence.

As I was about to descend the stairway, the mother of all jolts threw me against the bulkhead, drawing blood from my temple. I was stunned by the violence of the impact, yet remained standing. Again I shouted into the darkness: "Martín! Martín! Martín!" No answer. *Jeanne. Mathilde. Help me, my loves, I beseech you.*

"Answer me, Martín, please, answer me!" I yelled, terrified. "Answer me, damn you!"

My heart was beating fast, overcome with emotion. The tears on my face soon mixed with the ocean water. The deck below was now dangerously flooded. Any attempt at descending further was out of the question. I could do no more for my friend. The water was lapping at the top of the stairway. We were going to sink. The hull couldn't withstand the beating we had taken. I would never see Mathilde and Jeanne again, nor Mama, my friends, and family.

The ship settled level for a moment, and I took advantage of that to make my way back along the passageway as quickly as I could. Another jolt, less violent this time. I grasped the handrail and swiftly pulled myself up the stairway. Now I only had to make it to the end of the passageway. I could feel the wind whistling in my ears. In the distance I heard a door slam. A bit of light was filtering in from somewhere. I could make out shapes and shadows.

"Help!" I yelled.

"Is someone there?" came a barely audible voice from the darkness.

"Yes! I'm here! Where are you?"

A flash of lightning briefly lit up the whole passageway, and I saw a man sitting on the floor, a few yards from me.

"I'm here," he cried. "Help me, I'm hurt."

I crawled toward him, the rise of the ship slowing my progress. I felt his legs in the half-light and managed to open a door to our right, hoping for refuge.

"This way," I yelled, half dragging the man inside.

"Thanks!" he said as he sat down.

"What happened to the rest of the crew?" I asked.

"I don't know! When the bridge gave way and the water started coming in, they all rushed for the lifeboats. They must be dead by now!"

"And the captain?"

"No idea . . ."

"What shall we do?"

"Nothing. What do you want to do?"

"Get out of here!" I replied. "The ship's going to sink!"

He didn't say anything. Thunder growled in the distance. There was a bang as the door to the main deck opened then slammed shut in the wind. I thought hard for a few seconds. The man looked up at me, scanning my face as if trying to read my mind.

"Stay here," I said, "I'll be back soon." I dashed out into the passageway.

"Where are you going? Don't leave me here alone!" he implored like an abandoned child.

Ahead of me, the heavy door was still clanging in the wind. I approached it slowly, fearful of whatever horrors awaited me outside. Pushing it open, I surveyed the scene. An expanse of raging foam-capped waves stretched as far as I could see. The air was thick with a salty spray that stung my cheeks. Lightning zigzagged across the sky. The waves seemed unreal, exuberant, as if nature were determined to show us everything it was capable of. The ship's engines were inaudible above the crashing waves and howling wind. Indeed, I wondered if they were still working. There was nowhere to go. Even if I managed to get clear of the ship, I would surely drown. We were trapped. The sky was thick with clouds that shuttered out the moonlight. My moon had abandoned me. The crest of a wave broke over the top of the guardrail and struck me full on, nearly knocking me over. I managed to close the door tightly and slid down to the floor, where I leaned against the cold metal, feeling the vibrations as the elements battered the other side of it. We could only place our trust in the ship's solidity. If we sank, there would be no survivors. I returned to the cabin, where the injured man looked up at me expectantly.

"There's nothing to be done," I said sadly. "It's impossible to leave the ship without drowning."

This didn't seem like news to him. It was precisely because he had come to that same conclusion that he was still alive. I lay down on a damp bunk and closed my eyes, attempting to find refuge in a corner of my mind, sheltered by the apple trees of my childhood, close to Mathilde and Jeanne.

27

We were tossed about by the waves for several days and nights. How long exactly, I couldn't say. Time ceased to exist. I forced my eyes closed, trying not to dwell on it, while the other man puked his guts out, the foul odor filling the cabin. His incessant screaming interspersed with tears made me realize our species' inadequacy in the face of death. But his presence reassured me. Whenever he became really crazy, I hugged him so he'd quiet down—his anguished screams were making me nearly lose my mind too. Then he would curl up in a ball and sob quietly to himself until the madness seized him again.

During the day, I watched the ocean battlefield that extended into the distance, a mass of undulating foam and spray. The sky was nothing but a heavy curtain of gray mist. The sun had disappeared. Inside the ship, water was everywhere, running down walls and lamp housings. Its level rose a little each day, flooding the passageways, slowly smothering the metal beast, which was fighting a fierce rearguard action. Every time night cast its pitch-black cloak over us, I hoped I'd still be alive in the morning.

We stayed awake most of the time, night and day, and the lack of sleep made my head spin. Having nothing to eat and little to drink didn't help.

After a few days, it seemed like the ocean was calming down. The swell softened, the wind gradually eased. The other man had every appearance of a corpse in a coffin—white as a shroud, wide eyes staring at the ceiling. He hadn't screamed for a few hours. It was hot in the cabin, and the tropical humidity soothed my skin. I slipped into a deep sleep peppered with strange nightmares. A giant fish stood on deck, aiming a rifle at the crew and insulting the sailors in German. Hiding behind the bridge, I watched the scene, petrified. The fish ordered a man to come forward, in Spanish this time. Martín stepped out.

"Where is he?" yelled the scaly giant.

"He abandoned me in the passageway. He abandoned all of us: me, his father, his mother, his wife, his daughter, María, Catherine. He's a coward!" replied Martín, pointing a finger in my direction.

The whole crew turned to face me, smiling. My family and my friends. The fish glided toward me, his rifle aimed at my chest.

"Find the little German girl!"

Then he pulled the trigger.

I woke with a start and pawed at my chest, gasping for breath, my heart pounding. I looked around. The cabin was empty. A ray of sunlight shone through the porthole, softly caressing my face. I opened the round window and filled my lungs with fresh air. The sea was mirror smooth, reflecting a thousand points of sunlight and making me squint. The cyclone had passed. I was alive.

I walked up the passageway, taking care not to slip on the damp floor, and ventured out toward the bridge. A few sailors were gathered there, stunned by the desolation before them. The bridge had been ripped off, leaving a gaping hole into which the sea had poured. The ship was listing heavily to port, suggesting there was still a considerable amount of water in the hold. At the bow, a long section of guardrail had been swept away by the impact of the waves. The engines were silent. We were drifting at the mercy of the currents. There was no sign of any help on the horizon, only the flat blue expanse of the sea.

"Where's the captain?" cried one of the dozen sailors standing on deck.

Nobody replied.

"We need to radio a Mayday!" he went on. "Who knows how to work the radio?"

"It's broken, I already tried," replied another wearily.

"My God, what are we going to do? What stores do we have left?"

"Most of them are flooded, and the access passageways are blocked."

"What about fishing rods?" piped up a younger guy.

The others shook their heads.

"But we can find something to serve as a line, and there's plenty of wreckage up here we can use for poles. Everyone start looking and let's see what we can find. If we do nothing, we'll die!" This from one of the older crew, who was still clearheaded enough to take command.

We set to it, motivated by the idea of finding something to eat. We spent hours combing cupboards and lockers, all accessible passageways, first-aid kits, anything that might contain useful items. An awful stench hung in the air: the decomposing corpses of sailors drowned or fatally injured during the storm.

I made my way down a half-flooded passageway, pushing past several floating bodies. The smell was so bad I nearly vomited and had to cover my nose and breathe through my mouth. I reached a cabin, its door wide open. Inside I saw a corpse bobbing facedown on the surface of the water. I hurriedly rummaged through the upper lockers, wanting to spend as little time as possible in this place of death. Taking a deep breath, I plunged beneath the water to reach the lower lockers. As I turned to check the last one, something glinted in the sunlight streaming through the porthole, a slender silver chain hanging from the man's neck. In an instant I realized this was Martín floating in front of me on his belly, mouth wide open. A scream of terror emerged from my throat, sending a cascade of huge bubbles bursting to the surface. I grabbed my friend and turned him over so his mouth was out of the water, as if that could change anything. His face was puffy and swollen from the water and from being bashed about.

I retched, yellow bile spurting onto the surface of the water in front of me. The outgoing, effusive Spaniard, my best friend for over ten years, was now a lifeless, decomposing corpse. It was too much for me. I pushed through the water and back into the passageway. Once on deck, I stretched out and shakily inhaled the fresh air. My chest was constricted with sorrow for poor Martín. Above me, the sky was a cloudless blue. *Let me see Mathilde and Jeanne again,* I silently implored, feeling as if I had swum to the surface after spending a very long time underwater holding my breath.

Something clicked in my brain, reactivating long-dormant synapses. After swiftly running through the film of my childhood, I realized that my dream was not to become a sailor. It wasn't the freedom of a life on the ocean waves that had enchanted me when the sailor placed his hat on my head thirty years before, but the novel experience of a man treating me with warmth and kindness, something my father had obstinately refused me. In truth, my journeying across the oceans was a flight from the ghosts of my childhood, an attempt to forget that period of my life during which my heart was smashed countless times on the rocks of incomprehension. My dream was not to flee but to love—to be a good father to my daughter, whose own childhood I was missing out on. It was high time I looked after both her and Mathilde properly, whatever the cost. Praying that I would see them again and hold them close, I opened my eyes to life for the second time.

◆ ◆ ◆

A siren sounded in the distance. Turning to look, I saw a ship cutting through the sea in our direction. Had the heavens heard my prayer and granted me redemption, or was it yet another stroke of luck? I don't know. It doesn't matter. Everything is intertwined anyway. The other sailors began yelling and gesticulating wildly at the approaching vessel. We had all been granted a second chance.

FULL MOON

Sometimes, a delightful satisfaction awaits us at life's crossroads. It glides overhead, wings outstretched, and seems huge when viewed from below. Like that mythological bird I'd dreamed of as a kid, the phoenix reborn from its ashes, it bears us off heavenward to explore new horizons, new ways of thinking.

Up there the air is pure and the view, astounding. You're surprised to find yourself breathing calmly, daydreaming, savoring the sun's caress on your skin, the soft breeze, nothing but blue as far as the eye can see. Yesterday's storm has moved on. The torrential rains have stopped falling and now flow as a tranquil river.

Down on the ground, a few curious onlookers watch you, armed with binoculars, trying to decipher the mystery of this satisfaction. Others pay you no mind, caught up in the whirlwind of life that's weakening the craft they're paddling, often going nowhere.

You would love to stay up there and never know suffering again, listening to the murmur of stars being born, and contemplating the smile of the full moon. But the bird flies off into the distance and out of sight, in search of new prey to conquer, and the dark years return.

28

The next twenty-five years were the mellowest of my life. Not long after our repatriation, our ship was towed to the nearest port, where a marine-insurance expert inspected every inch of it. His verdict was indisputable. The vessel was deemed to have been so dilapidated even before the cyclone that it had been unsuitable for commercial use. The shipping company was ordered to make huge compensation payouts to the surviving sailors and the families of those who had perished, as well as to cover the retraining costs of those traumatized sailors who wished to pursue another profession. It was a notable victory of the proletariat over the bosses. The paradox was that we had plied the seas on that ship for ten years without anyone, be it the company, the captain, or the authorities, ever worrying about its obsolescence.

Of all the conclusions I had drawn from life, I was struck by one in particular. When it comes to money, man—this cognitive machine that adapts to survive—suddenly loses the ability to anticipate future catastrophes, ignoring the essential nature that has made him what he is. In these periods of forgetfulness or blindness caused by materialism, money distorts man's mind by short-circuiting his fraternal leanings, annihilating his foresight. We sailors were the victims of this narrow-minded capitalism, and it sickened me to think that if fate had dealt me a less fortunate hand, my daughter would have been deprived of a father and my wife of a husband.

In memory of my late friend Martín, I joined the resistance, so to speak, becoming a spearhead of this proletarian rebellion. I attended the various court cases and told the same story a thousand times to whoever would listen, be it the distraught jury or the appalled members of the press. Soon the affair became a national scandal. The shipping company tried to buy my silence, but I refused and denounced their attempts at corruption, which only added fuel to the controversy surrounding this tragedy. As a result, we were all compensated even more generously, which allowed me to put enough money aside to pay for my daughter's studies.

It was I who went to tell Martín's mother of her son's death; I insisted on it. The old lady, who lived alone in a gloomy apartment, stared at me with vacant eyes. She simply nodded without really taking it in, inoculated against grief by a life that had slipped through her fingers. When I handed her the compensation check a few months later, she simply put it in the pocket of her blouse out of habit.

Martín had been buried at sea, but we had a marble gravestone placed in a Bordeaux cemetery. On it I added a personal inscription: *To Martín, my best friend.* A fine rain streaked the face of the small memorial the day we dedicated it. Drops gathered in the indentations of the inscriptions before spilling over the edges. I laid a jasmine wreath in memory of his Carmen, that mysterious woman he'd told me about before he died.

True friendship is close to love, but without the carnal lust. I thought of all those nights spent with Martín in the privacy of our cabin, those stories he'd conjure to make his life seem more exciting. When night fell, he would talk without pause, gesturing wildly to illustrate his words. He smoked cigarettes by the porthole while sipping Rioja wine, for which he had a particular affection. Quite the character, that guy.

I recall us running through the streets of Las Palmas with María, like scared kids fleeing imaginary specters. Poor María, where was she now?

For a moment, the sight of his floating, swollen corpse came back to me. I felt choked with guilt at not having been able to save him. My dream where the giant fish shot me in the chest had haunted my nights ever since his death. Mathilde comforted me with all of her tenderness. My beautiful Mathilde, with her love whose source would never run dry. I shunted the image of his corpse from my mind. That wasn't the Martín I had known, the one singing, dancing, brimming with life. Tears ran down my face. I grasped Mathilde's hand, as well as Jeanne's, already a teenager. *"Gracias, amigo, que descanses en paz,"* I murmured. Then the three of us left the cemetery, walking toward our bright future together.

Shortly after I left the shipping company, Madame de Saint-Maixent, who was extremely well connected, introduced me to a local politician from the Bordeaux aristocracy, a man always impeccably dressed in the most elegant suits. He found me a job as head of security at the Bordeaux exhibition center. I easily found my feet in this new job, which afforded me the opportunity to sit and daydream when things weren't too busy.

Around that time I also began writing a book recounting the adventures of a sailor in love with the wide-open sea, a mixture of autobiography and fiction. When my family had gone to bed at night, I would sit in my quiet study, lit by a dim lamp, writing the exciting story of this reluctant hero of modern times. I loved my little nook, a corner of paradise where my creativity and imagination could run free. I enjoyed romanticizing my past. It provided a new equilibrium in my life, as if each letter, each line, each paragraph fed my thirst for self-expression. Then, when I was worn out by the intellectual effort and could write no more, I would slip into bed beside Mathilde's warm body and drift off to sleep, praying in the dark that this period of my life would never end.

◆ ◆ ◆

During those years, I also took advantage of the greater leisure my new job provided to make up for lost time with Jeanne.

Raising a child is a science, the theory and practice of which are like day and night, contradictory yet complementary. On paper, we sketch a perfect building with solid foundations in a style all our own. But when construction commences, nothing goes according to plan. A worker gets injured, there's a shortage of cement, the bricks are of poor quality, and a whole floor looks like it could collapse at any moment. We urgently review the plans and modify them as best we can, hoping the structure will hold. Sometimes the sumptuous palace we had imagined on paper turns out to be an ordinary dwelling, devoid of originality, blending into its surroundings. Sometimes it's the other way around, and as modest as the design appears on paper, it proves to be a masterpiece, envied by colleagues who lack such talent, such divine inspiration. And sometimes the sketch and the end result are similar, and we congratulate ourselves on having taken a more realistic approach, one without delusions of grandeur.

With Jeanne it was different. I had been absent far too long to have had much influence. Instead, Mathilde had been her primary role model. All I could do was attempt to tweak some of the details. But as the months passed, I finally managed to enter my daughter's world, to carve out a place for myself in her life and increase her esteem for me. I listened to her with interest, absorbed by what she said, never interrupting or dismissing her opinions, nor attempting to convince her otherwise. I built a relationship of trust with her, careful to do the opposite from my father. I didn't want my daughter to repeat my mistakes, to be bruised by adolescence, that key phase in the development of a human personality. I therefore redoubled my efforts and my vigilance as she grew older.

Sitting comfortably in my office one evening, my pen moving swiftly over the paper in front of me, I heard a gentle knocking at the door. I stopped writing and got up to open it. Jeanne was standing there in her pajamas, her eyes red from crying.

"What is it, my darling?" I asked, concerned.

"Papa, I'd like to talk to you about something."

"Of course, you can talk to me about anything you like. Sit down, I'll get you a blanket."

I pulled a thick quilt from a cupboard and wrapped it around her.

"So tell me, what's up?"

"I think I'm in love," she said, lowering her eyes.

"But that's wonderful—why are you crying?"

"Because this boy doesn't love me."

My daughter's face was pained. Teenagers often have a carefree look in their eyes that adults lose with age, gnawed at by the difficulties of daily life, the accumulation of disappointments and hardships. In the light from my little desk lamp, Jeanne resembled Mathilde as a young woman, patiently sewing under the tree in her garden. I was suddenly seized with anguish at the relentless passing of time, which either destroys or embellishes everything in its path—depending on your view. With superhuman effort, I managed to contain the tears of melancholy welling up inside me.

"How do you know he doesn't love you, Jeanne?" I asked, my voice trembling.

"He doesn't notice me, it's like I'm invisible."

"Is that sufficient proof he doesn't love you?"

My question troubled Jeanne. She looked up. Her almond eyes, so similar to my wife's, bored into mine. She thought for a few seconds, perhaps considering the situation from a new angle.

"Yes . . . Well, I think so. If he loved me, he'd look at no one else but me, as I do him!"

"Perhaps he doesn't behave the same way you do. Perhaps his way of loving is different from yours—he feels something for you but doesn't want to show it."

"You think?"

"Of course. Some people avoid other people's gaze for fear of being unmasked. Looking someone in the eye means exposing oneself, revealing one's fragilities. Some men hate doing that, my darling, because they don't want to show their sensitivity, their feminine side. It's frowned upon in the adult world."

"So maybe he loves me too?"

"That's for you to find out, by stimulating his buried feminine side," I said, praying that the boy in question was indeed in love with my daughter.

"How do you expect me to do that?"

"By letting your heart speak. Think of a way to make him understand what you feel."

"And if he doesn't love me?" she asked, embarrassed.

"At least you'll have tried your best. It will be painful at first, but that will pass and you'll come out of this experience stronger. And anyway, between you and me, how could anyone not love a girl like you? Look at you, you're magnificent, intelligent . . . If I were that boy, I wouldn't think twice, believe me!"

We both laughed. *What joy to see that smile on her face, to hear my daughter laugh,* I thought, very much the proud, happy father, a role that suited me perfectly. The study door opened and Mathilde popped her head in.

"What are you two scheming?" she asked roguishly.

"Nothing. We're simply talking, like two civilized adults."

Fresh peals of laughter emerged from the pair of us.

"You're just in time, Mathilde. I was going to tell Jeanne a story."

"A story?" Jeanne looked offended. "I'm too old for stories, Papa!"

"We're never too old for stories, my treasure, believe me." I smiled. "Sit down with us, Mathilde."

That evening I told my daughter about my childhood, my adolescence, my youthful dream of becoming a sailor, how I met her mother—who had also not paid any attention to me at first. I told her about the German officer, our encounter in the forest, his premature death, and the photograph of his daughter; my army service and Jean the actor, our trip to Frankfurt, my disappointment; then my voyage to Las Palmas, Martín, María, the pictures of her son, Manuel; my travels across the world, the cyclone that took my best friend's life; and finally, the book I was writing. Jeanne looked at me with admiring eyes, occasionally turning to her mother to confirm my retelling of various events. When I had finished, Jeanne—the girl who was "too old for stories"—plied me with questions, forgetting all about the boy she was in love with. She wanted nothing more than to know the end of my tale, and offered to help me find this Catherine Schäfer, whose trail I had lost in Spain.

"And María, what happened to her? We need to do all we can to find her, Papa. Your story is wonderful, worthy of a novel, you must write it!"

I smiled, recognizing in her eyes the same spark of life that glowed within me, the same drive to action, the same perseverance. Jeanne Vertune was a perfect mixture of her parents, at once calm yet passionate, intelligent yet naive, enigmatic yet expressive. Life had given me a priceless gift, a daughter with sparkling eyes who would carry the thread of love from which she herself was woven.

29

I was rounding a street corner in Bordeaux when I saw the poster. It was stuck in a shop window and depicted two grinning faces that seemed familiar. Beneath the photograph were the words:

Yes, Sir!
A STAGE PLAY
WRITTEN BY AND STARRING
JEAN BRISCA AND MARC DANTOUGE

Amazed, I realized these were my Paris actor friends. They were on tour across France and were performing their play in Bordeaux that very night, at a theater close by. I went straight to the box office and bought three tickets, aiming to surprise my two old friends by slipping backstage after the show and introducing them to Mathilde and Jeanne.

The afternoon seemed to drag by at a snail's pace. I couldn't wait to catch up with them after so many years. Both actors were now household names in France. I hoped that success had not changed their philosophy of life, now that they were part of the Paris showbiz set. I doubted that my two friends had gotten so bigheaded that they wouldn't recognize me or, worse, would ignore me. It wasn't their style. But I was a little apprehensive nonetheless.

We took our seats in the third row and waited for the play to begin. Jeanne seemed eager to discover another chapter of my story and, above all, meet two famous actors. She had brought a pen and a piece of paper for them to autograph so she could show off to her friends. The soft glow of the house lights illuminated her face, that of a radiant young woman. She had come through adolescence with no dramas or upsets, or at least that was the impression she gave. After all, most of an iceberg lies beneath the surface; you have to dive down to appreciate its shape. Fatherhood had taught me that we can never know everything about our children, however hard we try. We would love to uncover all of their mysteries, view their thoughts projected on a movie screen in order to anticipate any catastrophes and help them see the bigger picture with the benefit of experience. But that is impossible. They always retain some of their enigma, their hidden scars, joys, and pain.

The theater lights began to dim. Everyone quieted down as the curtain rose to reveal Jean dressed as our old drill sergeant. My friend had aged, his face lined from the energy and effort expended in so many performances, but he still retained his slender physique. As he began barking orders at the other actors, the whole theater erupted in laughter, Jeanne and Mathilde included. Jean really had captured Sergeant Major Lartigue's manner perfectly. I wondered what had become of him? Had life's long river spared him his portion of suffering? Was he still alive? I have always been intrigued by the paths people take in life. Sometimes I feel as if there's an invisible force pushing pieces around a huge chessboard, calculating millions of possibilities to achieve its ends. But one thing has always escaped me. What is the goal of this force? Its purpose? What does it mean for us humans, the pawns? I would like to understand the meaning of all this. But a cosmic energy situated billions of light-years away maintains tight control of the chessboard, resisting any attempt at discovery.

"Papa, are you OK?" whispered Jeanne.

"Yes, my darling, I was just thinking about something."

181

"Were you thinking about Catherine?"

"No. Don't worry. Watch the show."

Jeanne turned back to the stage, amused by my dreamy temperament. Marc and Jean had broken into a satirical ditty about the army. The audience laughed even harder. Their show was a crowd pleaser, of that there was no doubt.

As the show reached its climax, I realized I was watching my past unfold, or at least a version of it: the cruel drill sergeant found himself standing over two lifeless guys on the floor. The sound of approaching steps pounded from the loudspeakers. Not knowing what to do, the drill sergeant looked at the audience, terrified, then fainted. This comic stunt proved a hit, and there was a round of applause at this stroke of genius, which I had come up with twenty years before. I clapped loudly at this heartwarming nod to the past.

Jean and Marc took their bows. The theater emptied. I walked around the building to the stage door with Jeanne and Mathilde, and knocked.

A man appeared and looked me over. "What do you want?"

"I'd like to see Jean and Marc, please."

"So would everyone," he answered unkindly.

"Yes, but I'm an old friend of theirs from the army."

"Oh, that's a new one!" He sniggered. "A friend from the army . . . Yeah, right!"

He slammed the door in my face. I looked at Mathilde and Jeanne, who were dismayed at such rudeness. I knocked again. The same man reappeared.

"You again!"

"Listen, I swear I know Jean and Marc. Just tell them that Paul Vertune would like to see them, please."

"Paul Bertrune?"

"Vertune. *Ver-tune.*"

"Hang on." He sighed in annoyance and closed the door again.

We waited for several minutes in silence. Then the door suddenly opened wide and Jean Brisca appeared.

"Paul!" he cried. "What a wonderful surprise! How are you?"

He stepped forward and gave me a big, warm hug.

"I'm very well! And you, after all these years?" I replied, touched.

"I'm doing great, as you can see," he declared with a smile. "But who are these two lovely young ladies with you? Let me guess, the famous Mathilde?"

"Yes, pleased to meet you," said my wife, eyes wide.

"What a memory!" I replied in admiration. "And this is my daughter, Jeanne."

"What a beauty!" declared Jean. "Have you ever thought of becoming an actress, young lady?"

"Uh . . . no," answered Jeanne, a little flustered. "Pleased to meet you."

"Well, come on, let's go to my dressing room. Marc will be happy to see you!"

We followed Jean backstage to a small dressing room, where Marc was removing his makeup. He recognized me immediately and gave me a big hug too. They both autographed Jeanne's piece of paper, then we talked for a long time, recounting our respective lives since parting at Gare Montparnasse so many years before. The pair exuded such affection and kindness. Neither of them had changed. It was as if no time had passed at all.

"Did you ever find that German girl?" asked Marc.

"Ah, yes, the German girl!" added Jean.

"No, sadly not," I replied. "I picked up her trail in the Canary Islands, but she and her mother had moved on. That's all in the past now."

"Pity," said Jean, "I'd have liked to know what happened to them."

"To use in your next play?" I joked.

Jean and Marc both laughed. We exchanged telephone numbers and they invited us to come see them in Paris. Then we said our goodbyes and made our way home.

How wonderful to see that my two friends had retained their unshakable faith in life, their unimaginable optimism. The sparks in their eyes glimmered as brightly as ever. Here they were, earning a living, and a good one at that, off the artistic passions and dreams they had harbored since childhood. It made me very happy.

30

I finally completed my first novel after years of tireless work, whole nights spent writing, rewriting, and editing. A Bordeaux publisher took an interest in my manuscript and decided to publish it. As I walked down the street one day, I spied my book standing proudly on a wooden shelf in a bookstore window. I thought of my old schoolmaster, that short man with round spectacles and a thick beard who filled my brain with knowledge, and whom I had thanked posthumously at the end of my novel. The book earned me a small nest egg, which enabled me to take the two women in my life on vacation. We spent two weeks relaxing in Andalusia and enjoying the magnificent weather.

I was a man fulfilled in every way. My private life was idyllic. My professional life hardly excited me, but it did allow me to write novels in the evening. As a child, I could never have imagined such contentment, such satisfaction. Who would have bet a single franc on Paul Vertune, that kid with hands roughened from handling the wheat? I took stock of the path I'd taken, littered with obstacles, criticisms, and malice, but also joy and tender, loving moments. Existence is bipolar; it should be on medication.

Mathilde and Jeanne loved the Spanish way of life: the tapas and the streets full of smiling people recently freed from Franco's clutches. We even spent several days at the beach. Ever since returning from the Indian Ocean a few years before, I had avoided the sea as much as possible; the sight and smell of it evoked too many painful memories. But there was something magical about the beaches of Andalusia. The sun sat high in the sky, its rays reddening the skin of beachgoers, who were too busy building their sandcastles to care about sunburn.

"Papa, come join us!" yelled Jeanne.

I waved at her. "I'm coming!"

I got up from my towel, my body feeling languid from the sun's delicious caress, and strolled down to the two women sitting at the water's edge. The sea lapped gently at the soles of their feet, and they giggled like children as it tickled their toes. I sat down beside them on the wet sand and stretched out my legs. The water felt divine. And it was lovely to be there with Jeanne and Mathilde, far from the hustle and bustle of the city. It somehow bound us even closer together. We smiled at each other.

"It's like heaven here," Jeanne murmured.

"Yes it is," replied Mathilde.

"Papa?"

"Yes, darling?"

"Thank you for this vacation."

I would have liked to capture and store my daughter's words, Mathilde's smile, the sun warming our skin, the rippling waves, the bright-blue sky, the warm calm sea, the seagulls wheeling overhead, this chunk of my life in its entirety. I would have kept the bottle safe from prying eyes, in a lockbox, perhaps. And then, when nostalgia for bygone years overcame me, I would plunge my head into the container to experience it all again.

Happiness is fleeting, ephemeral. It's like a docile dog you keep close on its leash so it can't stray far—but then the animal shrugs off the leash and escapes. Happiness can't be tamed. It prefers to explore new horizons rather than get fat at the fireside. It allows you to stroke it before padding silently away. It will always find someone to stroke it. There is no shortage of eager hands.

All in all, happiness is much like us: eternally dissatisfied. It sat with us on that Andalusian beach, tongue hanging out of its mouth, meeting our gazes with adoring eyes. The three of us stroked its silky coat. But when we returned to Bordeaux a few days later, it took to its heels and disappeared again.

31

The telephone rang.

"Hello?"

"Paul?"

"Yes, who's calling?"

"It's Jacques."

"Jacques! How are you?"

"I need to tell you something." His voice was trembling.

"Yes?"

"Mama died this morning."

You never believe it at first. You try and persuade yourself the opposite. You try not to hear. *It's impossible. She can't be dead. I called her the day before yesterday and everything was fine.* It's unimaginable that the earth could continue to revolve for a single moment more without her. *It's not possible,* you repeat in an endless loop, *not possible, not possible . . .* Then, when doubt creeps in, when the repeated words start to lose their consistency, you begin to admit the terrifying truth. *Yes, it is possible.*

We always think we'll be prepared for the death of a loved one. Lying in bed at night, we'll run through different scenarios, imagining life without that person, attaching particular emotions and memories to them, hoping it will never happen, without for one moment admitting that fiction can become fact.

The day I learned of my mother's death, part of me died with her. I imagined Mama rising heavenward, trailing a white dress on which all my childhood memories were projected, like a movie screen. I saw us walking together as I clutched her hand tightly, so tightly. Then we were in the orchard at the family farm, stooping to pick up the fallen apples, our feet wet with the morning dew. The air was filled with a divine fragrance, a combination of my mother's scent and the fresh smell of the vegetable garden.

The projectionist changed reels and a new scene appeared, followed by another and another, the film suddenly accelerating until the images of my past began to blur. Tears ran down my cheeks.

I dropped the handset and slumped onto the sofa. I heard Jacques shouting my name over the phone: "Paul! Paul! Are you still there, Paul?" No, Paul wasn't still there. I'd been hit by an explosion of sadness. My chest was so tight with anguish I could barely breathe. My sobs filled the room.

Mathilde soon appeared, alerted by my cries of despair. She understood as soon as she saw me. I lay in her arms, trying to get some oxygen back in my lungs, gasping like a goldfish in a stagnant aquarium. Mama was dead. Flown away. Gone.

I sought sanctuary in my wife's embrace, drawing on all her kindness and love, that same love my mother gave me for years and which she would never give me again.

Mathilde, Jeanne, and I left the next morning, arriving in Sarzeau late that evening. Jacques was waiting for us on the dark station platform, hands in his pockets. He looked haggard, absorbed in thought, as if our mother's death had revived the forgotten ghosts of childhood, memories that had been scattered to the furthest recesses of his mind. As the train screeched to a halt, he stuck his fingers in his ears and grimaced.

When Jacques saw us alight from the train, he ran over, opening his arms with affection. He kissed Mathilde and Jeanne gallantly on their cheeks before giving me a big hug. I was surprised by this burst of humanity from my brother, who had spent most of his life repressing his emotions and controlling his behavior. He took our luggage to the car and we drove to his house, not far from the Vertune farm. Muriel, his wife, was sitting on the front steps smoking a cigarette. When her husband's car turned into the driveway, which was lined with flowerbeds, she stubbed out her cigarette on the ground and rushed to greet us. As inelegant and ungainly as she appeared, Muriel was an extremely kind woman, naturally outgoing in contrast to my brother's more withdrawn character. It was evident that their relationship was based on this balance between opposites. Jacques drew from his wife that openness to others he so sorely lacked, while Muriel drew from her husband his ability to contain and control his emotions in all situations.

Muriel hugged and kissed us, extending her deepest condolences, then she took our bags and Mathilde and Jeanne with her into the house. Later that evening, the five of us dined together, united in sadness. We said little, to the great discomfort of Muriel, who couldn't stand silence. When we were done eating, we politely thanked her. Jeanne and Mathilde went upstairs to bed, and after kissing her husband good night, Muriel followed them.

Jacques and I sat at the table, feeling awkward in the absence of our wives, who usually drove the conversation.

"Want a whisky?" asked Jacques. "I'm going to have one."

"Sure," I replied, thinking about our mother.

He went over to the grand mahogany sideboard that occupied nearly a whole wall of the living room, reached inside, and took out a nearly full bottle. He poured the amber liquid into two tumblers, which he placed on the table between us. Then he lit a cigarette.

"I didn't know you smoked," I said.

"From time to time," he replied. "For good occasions. And bad. Want one?"

Despite my disgust for tobacco—the cramped quarters aboard ship having been constantly filled with cigarette smoke—I surprised myself by accepting. Jacques lit it for me and I coughed at the first draw, the tip glowing red. He watched, amused, as the smoke wreathed around us, then he took a slug of whisky. A deafening silence filled the room, save for the ticking of the old clock.

"We're orphaned," he said, stroking the side of his tumbler with his finger.

"Yes."

"You really loved Mama, huh?"

"Yes . . . You didn't?"

"Of course I did," he replied, disconcerted. "But I mean, out of all of us, you were her favorite."

"I don't know. Anyway, none of that matters anymore."

Jacques knocked back the rest of his whisky in one go, grimacing as he did so. He seized the bottle and refilled his glass with the fiery, rough liquid.

"She talked about you a lot," he continued. "I think that in a certain way she never quite got used to you leaving. You were her little Paul. It was hard for her."

"For me too, Jacques."

"So why did you leave?"

There was a touch of reproach in his voice. Clearly my brother wanted to settle a score. For years he'd obviously been brooding over the memory of his young brother returning from his barracks and announcing he was leaving for Bordeaux to become a sailor. I had no desire to get into an argument, to lay out our family grievances on this day of mourning. But sometimes you simply have to grab your courage with both hands, or else the emotions stay hanging in midair like a storm about to burst.

191

"I left because there was nothing good for me here," I replied. "I wanted to escape the wheat fields.

"The wheat fields or Papa's memory?"

"Why are you asking me this, Jacques? Haven't we all suffered enough? Papa hated me since the day I was born. He always treated me like I was less than nothing! You think I'd love such a coldhearted father?"

"No, I . . ."

"You were the apple of his eye, the family favorite. You think it's easy for a kid to grow up in the shadow of his big brother?"

Jacques took another slug of whisky, then set his glass down. He hung his head, buried in memories of his childhood. The clock chimed, signaling that the time to settle life's scores had come. It would either scar us forever or offer a chance at redemption. We all have to face that moment sooner or later. Jacques lit another cigarette.

"It's true I wasn't always kind to you," he said.

"That's all in the past now," I replied, touched by his admission.

He poured himself a third glass of whisky, as if the alcohol gave him the strength to loosen the tangled knot of remorse deep inside him. He refilled my glass too.

"You know," he continued, "despite appearances, Papa wasn't always very kind to me either. He was strict and domineering. And unlike you, I had nobody to protect me."

"I know," I replied, "Mama always protected me from him. But I don't hold a grudge against anyone. I left to get away from all that."

"Yeah. I admire your courage." His gaze was lost in the depths of his whisky. "You're the only one who dared escape from here."

"Thanks."

"Did you like going to sea?"

"Yes, for a while. But now I look after Jeanne and Mathilde, and I'm much happier."

"So much the better." Jacques took a draw on his cigarette. "Tomorrow we'll bury Mama, and all the demons of our childhood with her."

"Indeed we will," I replied with a heavy heart. "Speaking of which, it's getting late, we should go to bed."

We got up and cleared the table of our glasses and the ashtray. There was a scent of nostalgia in the room, as if the past had left its fingerprints on the walls, the furniture, the floor, and the ceiling. My brother's jerky movements betrayed his inner torment, his regrets and remorse. I felt sorry for him but didn't know how to comfort him. The water of life had flowed under the bridge of our souls, patiently eroding its foundations yet smoothing the stone until all visible cracks had disappeared.

"See you tomorrow, Jacques." I headed for the stairs.

"Paul?"

"Yes?" I turned around.

Jacques walked toward me on unsteady legs, slightly breathless. He stopped in front of me, his eyes wet with tears. Was he finally going to say the words for which I'd been waiting so long? The words my father had never uttered, which he had taken to his grave for eternity? Jacques clearly wanted to speak, but his voice seemed to dry up before me, as if the words didn't want to leave his mouth, as if his vocal cords had seized up.

"Good night," he finally managed, and he gave me a hug.

"Good night, Jacques."

I went upstairs with a heavy tread. Jacques watched me from below. A hint of disappointment entered my mind; I managed to dispel it by thinking of the warm bed where Mathilde was waiting for me.

Experience teaches one to keep things in perspective. I was no longer in search of anything. I preferred to focus on my love for my wife and daughter rather than to continue hoping for kind words from my family. And Jacques had made an effort that evening. He had apologized for his behavior. It was a start. I slipped into bed and hugged my wife close.

I slept badly, scared of that moment the next day when I would see my mother's pale, lifeless corpse prepared for her final resting place. I recalled the image of my father lying in his coffin, the gaping hole in the village cemetery, and his cold body, which my brothers and I had stared at, more fascinated by death than sad at losing him. Now it was my mother's turn. The huge wheel of chance had stopped at her.

In the early morning, on our way to the funeral home, the colors of the passing landscape seemed muted. I saw places from my youth—the groves of trees, the tiled roofs, the little harbor with boats bobbing on the swell, the tall grasses in which my brothers and I had played, the fields where the ears of wheat stood proud. But in this backdrop so reminiscent of carefree times, there was something missing.

Mathilde's father was standing in front of the funeral home and I greeted him warmly, as I did my brothers, Guy and Pierre, my various cousins, and family friends. Everyone had come to pay their last respects to my late mother.

We entered the building's lobby, its walls darkly hued, only faint light coming through the drapes. I thought of the Indonesian funeral rites I'd once witnessed, where death was celebrated like a second birth, a prerequisite for a pleasant reincarnation. Everyone danced and sang. There were colors everywhere, nothing was black. Death was a beautiful thing there. Here it was different. Jeanne, standing stiffly beside me, clutched my hand.

"Are you ready, Papa?" she asked sweetly.

"Yes, I think so."

"Well, then, let's go."

A man showed us to the mortuary chapel where Mama was lying. We walked down a narrow corridor similar to the passageways on my ship where the corpses had piled up as the vessel was battered by the cyclone. There was an odd smell in the air, a smell of life's end, harsh and rough. The man opened a door and walked through, and our little group, my family and my brothers and their families, did too. As people filed into the room in front of me, my pulse began to race, my hands grew clammy, and my stomach started to knot.

Sometimes we are forced to face tragic circumstances, realities we cannot flee, even in our imagination. I would have liked a giant eagle to swoop down, dig its claws into my back, and carry me away from there, into the sky and clouds, far from that terrible scenario in which I had a starring role. I wanted to flee at all costs, flee the banality of that crushing situation, its lack of tact, its pain. I would have liked to be an astronaut walking on the surface of the moon, my beautiful moon shining in the night sky.

As I felt Jeanne pulling me into the room, I held my breath, like a diver plunging into the ocean's abyss.

32

Mama's face looked relaxed, like my father's when he was laid out. I stroked her pale skin and curled back a stray strand of hair that had fallen over her ear. My mother had been a stylish woman and would have never accepted people being left with a poor image of her.

I have always found death a strange thing to observe, as if the bodies lying before me would soon awake and go about their business like nothing had happened. A prank of sorts. I couldn't believe that everything ended there, at that moment, that it was all over for good. Maybe this was due to an error in my brain's logic circuits, or simply the leftover immaturity of a child who never wanted to grow up or stare reality in the face.

I kissed Mama's forehead and thought I heard her voice in the distance, calling my name, louder and louder: *Paul, Paul . . .* I listened carefully but couldn't tell where the sound was coming from. *Paul, Paul . . .* came my mother's voice again. Had I gone crazy? Was my imagination playing tricks on me? I was seized by an inexorable desire to run to her and join her for all eternity.

"I'll be back," I whispered to Mathilde, who looked at me strangely.

I briskly left the room and then the funeral home, guided by an irresistible force, as my mother's voice resonated far up in the light. I ran through the wheat fields, then took a muddy track, nearly falling flat on my face. Nothing could halt my progress, not the German officers demanding my papers, not the bombs exploding all around me, not the deafening crash of thunder over my ship. Nothing. I ran toward her, toward my mother, who was still alive somewhere out there.

I ran down the coast road, past the bobbing boats, then onto the tracks lined with thornbushes where she would pick blackberries for her tarts. After a few minutes of this mad dash, I recognized the dirt road of my childhood, the one leading to the washhouse, and I took it. There I found Mama, twirling around in a swirl of bubbles, and I stopped to admire her. She spun, arms outstretched, staring up at the sky, a smile lighting up her young, unlined face. I laughed too, like that child I still was. We always remain our mothers' children, whatever our ages.

It's strange how all the different periods of our lives can suddenly come together in our heads, as if time had lost its coherence, its reality.

My mother soon crumpled onto the soft, green grass, which covered the ground like a tablecloth spread for Sunday lunch. She lay there sighing with pleasure and exhaustion. Her bosom heaved as she breathed deeply, recovering from her efforts. Her skin was so soft and smooth. Her legs were folded beneath her. I frantically waved my hands, my palms violently striking together, as I applauded my mother one last time before she put on her outfit of wood and brass. She sat up in front of me, cross-legged, picked a daisy, and stuck it behind her ear. A sweet smile lit up her face.

"Paul, my darling, come sit by me, like when you were a little boy," she said in a soothing voice, beckoning me over.

I went and sat on the damp grass. The moisture penetrated my clothes, staining my good suit, but I didn't care. Men wear suits to hide their true identity, to mask their fragility, concealing themselves out of fear of being revealed. I've always hated wearing them.

"So that's it, Mama? It's the end this time?" I asked sadly.

"The end?" she replied. "It's just the beginning . . ."

"The beginning of what?"

197

"Of a new adventure . . ."

"But you're going away, you're leaving me all alone."

This didn't seem to trouble her. She simply placed a hand on my knee.

"I'll never leave you, my angel. Besides, Mathilde and Jeanne are here."

"Yes, but . . . what about you?" I asked, inconsolable.

"I have to go."

"I don't want you to."

"I must. Everyone goes someday."

"Not you, Mama."

"Yes, me too. But don't be scared, Paul. What binds us is stronger than death. People pass on, but their memories float in the air like clouds in the sky. You only have to be attentive to their presence, their smells, their magic. That's all."

"Mama?"

"Yes?"

"I love you."

"I love you, too, my darling."

The image of my mother slowly faded. Last to disappear was her face, illuminated by a new serenity, a wisdom to which only death knows the secret. She was soon no more than a mirage, then her outline dissipated like a sea fog in the rays of the rising sun. I found myself alone in a chaos of emotion.

I peeked over the edge of the low wall at the front of the washhouse and saw my face reflected on the smooth surface of the water. Wrinkles had formed everywhere, at the corners of my lips and eyes, across my forehead. My hairline was receding. The shadows under my eyes attested to long nights with little sleep, initially aboard ship, then in my writer's study. The skin on my neck was shriveling from the vicissitudes of life, like a chicken's wattle. The childish face that had smiled back at me from this expanse of water forty years before was now just a distant memory. I had grown old. But I felt less tormented, less affected by the emotions that had overwhelmed me as a kid, calmer now. What's curious about time is that it eats away at the skin of the fruit while purifying its core. *Youth is a beautiful thing*, I said to myself, *but old age is a well of knowledge, memories, and wisdom.* When you're a kid, you want to grow up fast. When you're older, you want to be a child again. I tell you, humanity has been built on a paradox since the very start. There's no logic to it.

I touched the icy water, sending ripples across its smooth surface. My reflection shivered in that liquid mirror. I plunged my hands down into the water, then splashed the walls of the old washhouse, laughing as I did so. I thought of Mama one last time as I paid her this most beautiful of homages.

Then I made my way back up the muddy track, a smile on my lips, to bury my mother in the village cemetery alongside her husband.

A few months after Mama's funeral, we had to decide what to do with the family farm. A realtor came to appraise the property and told me about a house nearby that was for sale for next to nothing. The owner was a rich Englishman with no children who only came once a year, and he wished to sell it as quickly as possible. The realtor showed us around the house, and when he told us the price, Mathilde and I looked at each other in astonishment. Two hours later, after phoning the bank, we were the happy owners of a vacation home in the Gulf of Morbihan. The Vertune farm, including all the fields, was sold to a farmer, since Jacques was now the village mayor and regional councilor, while my brothers had a joint fishing business, so we no longer had any use for the property. Upon our return to Bordeaux, Mathilde and I got our respective employers to give us some extra vacation time each summer so we could make the most of our second home.

33

In the early 1980s, Jeanne met the love of her life, married him, and soon got pregnant. Nine months later, a baby boy arrived. They named him François. Becoming grandparents was a new milestone for Mathilde and me. Childhood is a carefree time, adolescence is cruel, parenthood is a winding path on which you can easily slip, but grandparenthood is simply a pleasure.

Jeanne, who was now a lawyer in Bordeaux, left little François with us at our vacation home every summer. The little boy was growing up fast. He was tireless, curious, and always eager to learn, to explore different places and new fishing spots. He always had a big smile and asked a constant stream of questions.

"Grandpa, why do glowworms light up at night?"

"Because they capture sunlight all day long."

"Ah . . . And why do they do that?"

"Because it's their job to light up the night."

"Ah . . . Like car headlights?"

"Yes, except it's more natural and doesn't hurt your eyes as much."

François nodded, convinced that my explanations were true. He meditated on this for a while. Then, with the information securely stored away in his head, he resumed his questions with even greater intensity.

"So if we put glowworms in car headlights, maybe they would hurt our eyes less?"

"It's possible . . . But they wouldn't provide enough light, and there'd be accidents."

"Hm . . . Well, then, if we put thousands of them in headlights, maybe that would work, Grandpa?"

"Yes, maybe," I replied with a smile.

François was a quick learner, and he surprised me more every year. One evening, when we were walking back from the little port of Logéo together, he stopped on the hard-surfaced path that ran along the beach, now covered by high tide.

"Grandpa, who's Catherine?" he asked, his eyes shining.

I was at a loss for words.

"Uh . . . She's a friend," I replied, my voice quavering.

"Mama told me a story about Catherine and María, and said they were in Spain and looking for a little girl in a port."

"Yes, I told Mama a story like that when she was young."

"Grandpa?"

"Yes, my darling?"

"Do you think they'll find the little girl in Spain one day?" he asked sadly.

I felt a pang as I thought of the German officer lying dead on the ground, the picture of Catherine, the old lady in Frankfurt, and Martín's and my encounter with María in Las Palmas.

"Of course they'll find her."

"Mama told me the story ends in the port and that's it," he retorted.

"That's because she's forgotten it," I said, without figuring on the kid's intelligence.

"Do you know the ending, Grandpa?"

No, I didn't know it. Over the course of these many years, time had gradually erased the memory of the little girl in the photograph, along with María's features. In my grandson's eyes I saw all of the mystery surrounding this business, all of the concern at not being able to bring it to a close, to reach a happy ending. Children need to be able to dream the things that adults bury with time. François had revived the old demons in me. Through him, something of my youth had returned.

I didn't want to invent another chapter. I didn't want to lie to him. So I didn't answer. We returned home, each of us lost in thought, deprived of a happy ending that would have delighted the both of us that evening. I went to bed hoping that one day I'd complete the quest I'd undertaken as a young man. But how? The whole business was just a distant memory, a hope abandoned like so many others.

34

Mathilde and I were strolling through the park in Bordeaux, as we did each Sunday. It provided an opportunity to chat about our life. We were recently retired, spending half the year in Bordeaux to be close to our daughter and the other half at our second home in the Gulf of Morbihan. We were happy, she and I. Forty years together, that's something. The roots of our love were stronger than those of a thousand-year-old baobab tree. Love is one of the most beautiful things on earth, and it's the only way to attain a deep sense of fulfillment and achieve the wisdom that lies so far beyond the everyday futilities that pollute our existence.

Mathilde suddenly stumbled. I caught her before she fell.

"Is everything all right, my love?" I asked with concern.

"My head's spinning. I'd like to go home," she replied.

We did so, and I helped her into bed. She soon fell asleep, feverish. *Probably a chill,* I thought.

The next day, her state had not improved, and I decided to call the doctor to our home. Seeing his patient half-conscious, he had her taken to the hospital immediately. We went in an ambulance, sirens wailing, those same sirens you hear as you walk down the street and wince as you think of the poor person stretched out inside. This time, the victim was Mathilde, my wife, my reason for living. I sensed my existence waver on its pedestal, then crumble piece by piece. Once again, the Grim Reaper loomed on the horizon, ready to cut down anything in its way, with no regard for age.

At the hospital, Mathilde was given a whole battery of tests, those real-world things I've never been able to wrap my head around. After a few hours of unbearable waiting interspersed with cups of coffee, a man in a white coat appeared and beckoned me to follow him. We entered a white room with only a couple of pieces of basic furniture. On the man's desk were some photographs of people—his wife and children, no doubt.

"Please sit down, Monsieur Vertune," he said nervously.

"Thank you," I replied, taking a seat.

"How are you?"

"A little anxious, I must admit."

"Yes," he said, looking into my eyes. "I understand."

"How's my wife?"

"She's resting at the moment."

"Good. When will she be able to leave?"

"Monsieur Vertune, there's something I have to tell you."

"Yes?"

"We gave your wife an extensive series of tests."

"And?"

The man got up and placed an X-ray image against an illuminated box. I thought I could make out a human skull. He took a little stick in his right hand and pointed at something on the image.

"See this patch here?"

"Yes."

"That is a malignant tumor, Monsieur Vertune, in your wife's brain."

"A tumor?" I replied with horror.

"Yes."

"Cancer, you mean?"

"Yes."

"Is it serious?"

"Listen, I must be straight with you. The tumor is located in an inaccessible part of the brain. It's inoperable. We can do nothing for her."

"There's no possible treatment?" I asked, in shock.

"Chemotherapy might kill her at her age, and the chances of it doing any good are minimal, if not zero."

"So does that mean she has no chance?"

"None, Monsieur Vertune, I'm very sorry."

"How long does she have left?"

"Two months at the most. The tumor is very advanced. I'm terribly sorry, we can do nothing for her."

I looked up at the image of my wife's head on the screen, and that huge white patch. Two months. How was it possible? What act of cruelty had I committed to deserve this? Death had taken my father, my best friend, my mother, and was now after my wife. Why was I the target of such misfortune? What would I become without her, my Mathilde, my golden-fingered seamstress?

I went home in a desperate state of mind, hoping that the doctor's diagnosis was a huge mistake. She wasn't so old, after all. We had so many things left to do together, so many moments left to share. I wanted to show Mathilde this vast world that I had seen during my years at sea: the smiles of the Indonesian people; the carnival drums in Rio de Janeiro; the sun-kissed beaches of Fuerteventura, where the locals gathered around barbecues come evening. Life's long hourglass was still running. Mathilde couldn't die now; it was simply impossible. Her eternal optimism would conquer the evil silently eating away at her brain. We would soon head back to our native Brittany, where we'd welcome our grandson again come summer, frolicking joyfully with him in the wheat fields. The three of us would picnic on the beach and dig for clams; we'd gather crabs, periwinkles, and other shellfish for the feast that was Sunday lunch. We would swim as far as the wooden posts off Kerassel beach that marked the edges of the oyster beds—in my childhood we used to race each other there. Mathilde would have fun with her grandson, preparing his snacks even though he was nearly a teenager, and picking raspberries with him. She'd come out to the garden to fetch us, calling, "Dinner!" with a big smile on her face. She'd walk with us to Logéo port in the dreamy summer twilight and cut reeds to make peashooters, as the majestic moon winked at us kindly from up in the sky. Mathilde couldn't die. She was immortal. This was all just an awfully bad joke.

I went to see my wife every morning and stayed close to her all day and into the evening, accompanied by Jeanne, who took time off from work. Initially I did think the diagnosis was in error; Mathilde felt very well and walked around the park adjoining the hospital without any problems. Against her doctors' advice, she wanted to try chemotherapy and then radiation therapy—barbaric concepts that only white-coated doctors understand, not ignoramuses like me. Little by little, the attacks of dizziness became increasingly frequent, the nausea ever stronger, the screaming more and more terrifying. Mathilde frightened me. Her existence was wavering—of that there was no doubt.

In the evenings, when I returned from the hospital, I went to sit in the garden. Our vegetable patch, planted with great care by my wife's green fingers, impatiently awaited her return. Mathilde loved this little plot of earth above all else—it reminded her of the wide-open spaces of Brittany. She had spent many happy moments there, her hands covered with dark soil, sweating streams when the sun was out. I contemplated her masterpiece, devastated at my having to navigate this ocean of illness without a rudder.

One day, while I was sitting with her, the doctor asked me to step outside for a moment.

"We're stopping the treatment, Monsieur Vertune," he said with that implacable scientific logic I hate more than anything.

"Very well," I replied, understanding that the relentless therapies no longer served any purpose.

"She only has a few days left. Take her somewhere that is dear to her, where she can live out her remaining days peacefully. The hospital can rent you a wheelchair if you wish."

I wanted to slap him, to thrash him as the inhabitants of my village did the German soldiers. Capitalism displays all of its cruelty, ignominy, and barbarism, even at life's darkest moments. One day, the balance of the world will undergo a seismic shift, and humanism will topple the sickening dictatorship of profitability. But the stirring of such awareness is not yet in the cards.

We settled Mathilde in a wheelchair and left the hospital.

On the horizon, the pale sun dropped slowly into the sea, capitulating as it did every evening. There was no one about by the little creek near the port of Logéo. I had taken Mathilde back to the landscape of her childhood. She hadn't spoken for several days; her vocal cords had given up, as had her limbs. Here we were, by that same creek where I had asked for her hand forty-three years earlier. We'd been so young at the time, full of energy and drive. The future lay wide open before us. But life had zipped past without pause. Not a single speck of grit had slipped into its gears to block its progress. Yet we enjoyed the view all the same. We sat, Mathilde in her metal chair, I on the sand. I held her hand tightly. We had accomplished so much together, the two of us.

"I've been so happy with you all these years, Mathilde," I said, not expecting a reply. Nor was there one. Mathilde was too frail to speak. Yet I know she heard me.

That night, Mathilde passed away. We buried her close to her mother in the village cemetery where my parents also lay. Monsieur Blanchart, who had such energy that death didn't dare approach him, cried silently beside me. His daughter's cruel fate reflected that of his wife, as if cancer is handed down from generation to generation like a sinister inheritance. I thought about the little seamstress sitting in the shade of her tree, with her spools of thread and her needles. Jeanne and François cried too. As for me, I wandered like a shadow amid the ruins of our life together. The day Mathilde died, I lost my smile, the smile people had reproached me for all my life, the smile I had worn since the day of my birth.

35

There I was. Or rather, there my body was. My mind was elsewhere, lost somewhere on the horizon. The ocean, my playground, my past, stretched out as far as I could see. I was rooted in the big blue just like a tree was rooted in the dark earth. There was something magical about the ocean, something unexplainable, irrational. Every time my energy was diminished, I recharged my soul's battery by contemplating the ocean's vastness, as waves lapped at the beach.

Often I had wondered if any other part of nature could be more beautiful than my ocean, without ever finding an answer. I had spent fifteen years aboard cargo ships seeking answers to life in its currents, its swells and breakers, before finally realizing that the truth was always out of reach. So I had abandoned the ocean, sickened by its inconsistency, its hazards. But now everything was different. Mathilde was dead, and I eagerly returned to the seashore to feast my eyes on its beauty, to somehow fill the gaping hole inside left by my wife's death. Truth be told, this dance of the natural elements in perpetual motion intoxicated me as wine did a drunkard. I had become addicted to its salty spray, its briny tang, its heaving swell and huge rollers. I watched it for hours, sitting on the sand, alone. It had been the same routine every day since Mathilde's death. I got up around nine o'clock in the morning, had breakfast, then went to sit on the beach until twilight. I came every day, no matter the weather—rain, wind, sun, or clouds—forgetting to live. Every day that dawned was as fresh as a ripe fruit plucked from the tree. I tried to think of nothing—or rather I avoided thinking about Mathilde at all costs. The slightest misplaced thought triggered a torrent of tears, and grief wrenched at my gut.

I would see people on the beach walking with their feet in the water. They threw bread to the birds and were delighted every time one dived down to snatch a morsel. I sometimes wondered which of the two species was feeding the other. Some of the people waved to me, but I didn't wave back, too preoccupied with not thinking, with escaping hostile reality.

When night fell, I sometimes caught a glimpse of my beloved moon, my full and silent moon, peeping out from behind a cloud, and I smiled at it, at it alone. The moon had been my companion since childhood, and I had a great respect for it, almost cultlike, similar to the Inca with the sun. Contrary to its daytime opposite—proud, arrogant, burning bright with a thousand flames—I found the moon to be calmer, discreet, and soothing. The moon has no need to shine as brightly, no need to be so boastful. It simply glides across the sky at night while the whole world sleeps, without ostentation or prestige, a friend to insomniacs. You can look at it without hurting your eyes, unlike the sun, which blasts your retinas if you try to pierce its mysteries. The moon was my divinity. It soothed my soul's torments with its pale reflections off the sea, its subtle craters, the many shapes it assumed in the course of its cycles, like those of my personality. I identified with the moon. My moon. My childhood pebble perched up in the sky.

Finally, when the temperature fell and I started to get cold, I returned home, where I lay on the bed and dreamed of my Mathilde when she was still alive, the meals she'd spend all afternoon cooking, her bursts of laughter under the summer apple trees in the garden, our love that had known no limits.

Jeanne worried about me. She called and I assured her that everything was well. The mourning period is a time to appreciate solitude. My daughter encouraged me to start writing again, but I didn't see the point. My source of inspiration had dried up. Mathilde hadn't just been my wife, she was also my muse.

I spent one long year like that, just staring at the ocean. And I could happily have continued to do so for the rest of my life, so as not to have to think about anything, to join my wife as soon as possible. But once again, destiny wasn't interested in what I wanted. It suddenly collared me and dragged me back to reality. *Your life isn't over,* it seemed to be saying.

36

Kerassel, Morbihan, 1992

I was resting on my bed one evening when the doorbell rang. It gave me a bit of a shock, since I wasn't expecting anyone. My bedside clock said *8:30 p.m.* I got up in the half-light and peered out the window. A brown-haired man, around forty years old, was standing on my doorstep in a spotless suit. He didn't look like anyone I knew. *Must be a salesman,* I thought. Throwing on a jacket, I went to open the door and found myself facing a beaming smile.

"Good day, Mr. Vertune," said the man, in a Spanish accent.

"Hello. Can I help you?"

"Yes," he replied, looking me straight in the eye. "I want to thank you."

"What do you mean?"

"Thank you with all my heart," he said, bursting into tears.

The man fell to his knees and grasped my legs. I glanced up and down the street to make sure no one was witnessing this embarrassing scene. He sobbed as he clung to me, his forehead pressed to my thighs. Who was this man? And why was he behaving in this way? He was clearly quite distraught, and it pained me.

"Come in, please." I helped him to his feet.

I grasped his arm and led him into my living room. He sat on a sofa with his head in his hands, trying to hold back muffled sobs. I handed him a tissue.

"What's the matter?" I asked sympathetically.

"I'm sorry," he stammered. "It's nothing, just that seeing you . . . it's so emotional."

"Seeing me? What do you mean?"

"You don't recognize me?"

"I don't. Who are you?"

The man dried his tears, pulled himself together a little, and leaned back on the sofa. I had never seen him before, I was sure of it. What on earth was he doing in my living room?

"You sure you don't recognize me, Monsieur Vertune?"

"No, I don't think so, are you a friend of Martín?" I replied, realizing that his accent was similar to that of my deceased friend.

"No, I do not know this Martín."

"So who are you?"

"I am Manuel, the son of María."

I froze. For a second it seemed like my heart had stopped and that the blood in my veins had ceased to flow. María's son? The child of a mother forced to work the streets of Las Palmas? I couldn't believe my eyes. I scrutinized him for a few seconds. Gradually his mother's features became apparent: same eyes, same lips, same round face.

I touched his cheek. "Ma . . . Ma . . . Manuel."

He smiled shyly. "Yes, Monsieur Vertune."

"How on earth did you find me? And where's your mother? What has happened over all these years? Where were you?" I cried, desperate for answers after so long.

"It is a very long story, Monsieur Vertune. But before I tell you, can I please have a glass of water?"

"Of course," I said, going to the kitchen and returning with the water.

"I am sorry for crying, Monsieur Vertune, but so many memories come when I see you."

"It's quite understandable, but please call me Paul."

"Very well . . . Paul. Your neighbor in Bordeaux, she give me your address here. It was a long journey.

"And María?" I asked impatiently.

Manuel's face immediately grew sad. I realized that my question had stirred up deeply buried pain.

"My mother came back one day when I was little. She was happy. I remember that day like yesterday. I was in the garden at my grandparents' house in Málaga, and she appeared and ran to me. She took me in her arms and promised never to leave me again."

Manuel's gaze was lost in those memories. His voice held the same nostalgia that I felt in recalling my own memories, the memories of my entire life, of María, of Mathilde, of all the encounters that had made me the man I was.

"She spoke about you a lot, Paul, about your meeting on Alcaravaneras Beach. I went there last year. It is a beautiful beach."

"How come you speak French?" I asked, intrigued.

"I went to French school in Málaga. It was a way for my mother to thank you for what you did for us. That is why I speak French now. Well . . . I try . . ."

"You speak it very well. Better than my Spanish."

Manuel smiled.

"When I was a teenager, my mother, she told me the story of Catherine Schäfer. She kept the little photograph of the German girl, the photograph you put in the envelope in Bordeaux."

"Ah, yes?"

"Time passed, and she started to feel guilty because she could not help you with your search. She could not sleep at night. She told me again and again that you helped her even though it was dangerous for you, and that she felt bad because she was not able to help you too."

"But I didn't expect anything from her in return."

"I know. But my mother wanted to find the German girl. She telephoned everywhere in Las Palmas for the information: hotels, the *ayuntamiento*, how you say?"

"*Ayuntamiento*? The town hall."

"Yes, the town hall. She was obsessed with helping you. She wanted to make a surprise to thank you for what you did for her."

"Did she find out anything?"

"From Málaga, it was difficult to find information. So one day she went there."

"To Las Palmas?"

"Yes. She did everything possible. She even hired a private detective with the money she saved. She did everything to find the German girl."

He pulled a bunch of envelopes from his jacket pocket.

"Here is all the letters she wrote me in that year, 1965. She described all her searches. But after some months she did not find much information, so she went to see her old colleagues." Manuel looked ill at ease. "I only discovered this later. But I did not blame her for that. My mother . . . she was a wonderful person." He smiled again. "One of the prostitutes at the port recognized her and told her to go to this house in the quarter of La Isleta. She went there. Then I never heard anything from her again."

"Do you know what happened to her?" I asked, horrified.

"On the last letter she sent me, she put the address of the house. I went there two months later because I was worried about having no news."

"And what happened?"

"A man opened the door and I asked him if he had seen my mother. He invited me into the house, then he hit me very hard. When I woke up, I was tied to a chair. There was blood all on my shirt. The man stood there and he asked me questions about my mother and the mother of Catherine. He wanted to know why everybody look for them. Then he left and I was alone in the room. I screamed and screamed for a long time, and then the neighbor, he called the police."

"Who was the man?"

"He was the man who . . . who . . . My mother and her colleagues, they work for him, you understand?"

"Yes, he was their pimp."

"I think the man, he did not like that she escaped ten years before, and when he saw her again he killed her, like he killed the mother of Catherine, because she also wanted to escape. The police, they found three bodies in the . . . under the house, three women's bodies. The women, they were in . . . how you say, *cemento* . . . ? Is hard, like stone . . . ?"

"Cement."

Yes, *cemento*, they were in the *cemento* with all their things, their clothes, everything. That is why she did not give me any news. We took my mother back to Málaga and we buried her there."

"I am so sorry, Manuel, that's just awful, awful. All that is my fault . . ."

"No. It is the fault of nobody. My mother, she had faith in life, faith in you, Paul. She just wanted to help you, like you helped her."

A long silence filled the room. I thought of beautiful María, defying danger to find the German girl for me in order to repay my help. I felt guilty about having involved her in all this business by slipping her Catherine Schäfer's picture in order to rid myself of my cumbersome past. That harmless gesture had plunged her into a fruitless quest. I'd often felt angry at not hearing from her, assuming a kind of ingratitude on her part, without knowing the terrible truth. María had been dead all those years, like Martín, my mother, and now Mathilde. The bodies piled up in my twilight years, and every day, I realized a little more how incapable I was of controlling the phenomenon.

"There is another thing I must tell you, Paul."

"What?" I replied sadly.

"When I returned to Málaga, after I buried my mother, I joined the police. Maybe to get revenge for her death, who knows? I worked hard and I became a detective. But I thought about that Catherine Schäfer for many years. And then a couple of months ago I returned to Las Palmas for vacation and to remember my mother. I visited the whole island, I went everywhere, it is *magnífico*!"

"Sadly, I only visited Las Palmas."

"Ah, that is a pity. You must go see Roque Nublo, this big rock, so big, up in the mountains. You can see all of the different Canary Islands from there when the weather is good. *Magnífico*. Well, I went to the police station and I showed them my detective badge, and they allowed me to look in their archives. I found the information about the case and all the evidence, which was not much. But there was this small plastic bag, and inside there was the photograph of Catherine Schäfer and your address. I put them in my pocket, and that is how I found you! Here, I give them back to you."

He handed me the little black-and-white picture of the German girl, which brought back memories of my childhood, the liberation, the killing of the German soldiers in the village square, Mathilde's smile. I felt a twinge in my heart.

"One last thing," Manuel continued. "In the plastic bag, from the mother of Catherine Schäfer, there was a rent receipt with her address. She did not live in the quarter of La Isleta but nearby, in Guanarteme, opposite Las Canteras Beach. I went there. An old woman, she opened the door. She told me she owned the house for forty years. She rented a room to people who stayed a short time. She remembered very well the German woman, Martha, she told me."

"Yes, Martha, that's her!" I said, thinking of the nameplate on the building in Frankfurt.

"She told me Martha had a daughter, Catherine. And that Martha was saving money to go to Argentina. She had friends there who could help her."

"Argentina?"

"Yes. When Martha disappeared, the old lady, she found the address of the friends in Argentina and she wrote them. They replied after a few weeks and said to send the daughter to them. She did this, with the money Martha saved."

"So Catherine Schäfer has been in Argentina all these years?"

"Yes. And you know what? I telephoned the Spanish consulate in Argentina, pretending I needed information for an investigation about Catherine Schäfer. Two weeks later they sent me this envelope. Take it, Paul."

I took the envelope, slipped my fingers inside, and withdrew a piece of paper. It was written in Spanish, but in the middle of the text there was an address: *Catherine Schäfer, 180 Avenida Luis María Campos, Buenos Aires.*

"Is she still alive?" I asked.

"Yes. *La vida da muchas vueltas,*" he said with a smile. "Life, it is full of surprises."

"Thank you, Manuel."

"Thank you for saving my mother, Paul."

The past suddenly resurfaced, all those questions that had remained unanswered, all those moments left up in the air. Life was offering me a fresh chance to make good on a promise I'd made when I was a child so many decades ago. I only regretted that Mathilde and Martín were no longer alive to share my joy at completing my quest.

I called my daughter and told her the story. She was astonished. Manuel stayed the night at my place and left in the early hours, after giving me a big hug. He invited me to vacation with him in Andalusia, where I would be received as a king in memory of my friendship with his mother. The next day, I bought three plane tickets to Buenos Aires. Jeanne and François would come with me. Finally I would be able to bring this whole story to a close. My grandson would be happy.

37

The plane flew over the ocean. Looking out the window, I could make out tiny white dots here and there, the lights of ships. Their crews must have been sleeping at that hour, and I hoped that the swell was being gentle with them. François snoozed peacefully beside me, the tired little boy's head resting against my arm. Jeanne was reading a book. From time to time she would glance at her son and adjust his blanket.

It's funny, but although I had seen much of the world during my many years at sea, this was my very first time flying, and it fascinated me. Here we were, over thirty thousand feet high, traveling at astonishing speed. At takeoff, I had been surprised by the plane's power, the noise of its engines, its violent acceleration in taking to the air. I watched the landscape pass beneath us, mesmerized by the earth's beauty from above: meandering rivers sculpted into the rock, huge mountains looking like lowly hills. Then, as we left land behind and I saw the Atlantic, I was filled with a surge of emotion as I thought of my former life on the ocean waves. I recognized the Strait of Gibraltar, the coast of Morocco, and, further on, the Canary Islands.

As we flew over the rounded rocky shape of Gran Canaria, the view was superb. I thought about María and Martín, the three of us running through the streets of Las Palmas. *Time goes by so fast,* I thought. The chapters of the book of life follow each other ceaselessly, the pages turning before we can reread the important passages.

Night was falling, the horizon darkening, drawing its infinite blanket of stars over our heads. The moon seemed suspended in the sky, levitating. It was full, as full as my life, my joys and hardships, my dreams and renunciations, my glories and failures. I missed Mathilde. She was the main absence on this trip, she who had been so interested in my story. *I'll return to writing sooner or later*, I thought. I wondered if Catherine Schäfer really lived at this address, if there hadn't been a mistake, if it was someone else with the same name. I hadn't had the courage to call the number, for fear of disappointment. And anyway, I'd been wanting to discover Argentina for some time, so I figured I might as well kill two birds with one stone.

A stewardess walked down the aisle and offered me a beverage; her hair was up in a bun, and there was laughter in her almond eyes. I declined her kind offer and dozed off, dreaming of my wife, my sweet wife sitting up there in heaven.

The plane landed a few hours later. François and Jeanne were now awake beside me. Though the boy had slept all through the flight, like me, he was impatient to know the end of the story. We touched down rather hard, shaking the passengers, who applauded, reassured to be on the ground again. After retrieving our luggage, we walked outside to be greeted by a horde of taxi drivers shouting at us, each boasting the merits of their own cheap and fast service. Jeanne, who spoke Spanish, negotiated a price with one of them, and we drove to our hotel along a traffic-clogged highway. Our driver chattered away without pause, and Jeanne politely agreed with everything he said, hoping he'd eventually shut up. On the edge of the city was a vast shantytown: rickety sheet-metal roofs and huge piles of garbage,

221

the stench, considerable. The inhabitants, disadvantaged by a cruel accident of birth, attempted to eke out a living as best they could amid the filth of these slums, the kind of people you see on street corners and cruelly ignore as you pass by. Yet it's not really them we're scared of, but the reminder that a twist of fate could put us in their shoes, on the streets without a penny to our names. In order to flee this reality, we adhere to a code of silence that nobody dares break.

The taxi stopped at a red light as we entered town. A disabled man stumbled between the cars, supporting himself with a pair of crutches. The drivers ignored him when he knocked on their windows, not even deigning to look at him or give him the slightest token of compassion. The taxi moved off as soon as the light turned green, as if offering us a chance to escape this miserable man, whom the bloodred traffic light had forced us to look at for a few moments.

"Buenos Aires," said the driver, pointing at the avenue we were driving down. "Avenida Nueve de Julio!"

"*Gracias,*" I replied.

We turned onto a side street, then made several more turns onto identical-looking streets before drawing up in front of our hotel.

"*¡Ya estamos, chicos!*"[2] he said, proud of himself.

"*Gracias,*" I answered again.

Inside the hotel, the receptionist took our passports and handed us the keys to our rooms. I asked her politely if Catherine Schäfer's address was far from here. She replied that it was just a few blocks away. We went up to our rooms and rested for a few hours.

That evening, I took my daughter and grandson to a restaurant where tango dancers put on the most beautiful show. We clapped, enraptured by their graceful performance. Then we returned to our hotel and slept. A big day awaited us.

---

2   Translation: "Here we are, kids!"

38

It was very hot that next day. The sun beat down on the Argentinean capital, turning the city into an oven. We spent the morning walking through the streets of Buenos Aires, which were filled with impressive jacaranda trees that tinged everything mauve. They delighted François, and he scampered among the blossoms that had fallen on the sidewalk. A few street musicians were playing here and there, happy to be living freely despite their precarious financial situations. *This is a nice place to live,* I thought.

In the afternoon we decided to head toward the address Manuel had given us. As we turned onto the Avenida Luis María Campos, I felt all the weight of the years settle on my shoulders, all those encounters, all those paths taken, all those choices, all those moods. The air was full of the sweet scent of the jacaranda blooms drying in the sun. When we reached number 180, my legs wobbled and I had to grab hold of a doorway so as not to fall. Jeanne took my arm.

"Are you OK, Papa?" she asked.

"I'm scared, Jeanne," I replied, anxiety gripping my chest.

"Shall we leave? It's fine if you want to . . ."

"No, I want to see her. But I'm scared that it'll bring everything back. All these years spent looking for her, all those people I met along the way. I'm scared she won't want to listen to me. Or, worse, that she simply won't care about the whole stupid business."

My daughter, who increasingly resembled her mother, looked me straight in the eye.

"Papa, this has been such an important part of your life. It doesn't matter what happens today, you'll have pursued your dream as far as you could, like you always have. We're all so proud of you."

I remembered María's face when we had docked in Bordeaux, beautiful María paralyzed with fear at the idea of seeing her son again. I had gently reassured her, just like my daughter was doing now. Roles are never etched in stone. They vary according to the situation.

"And my father, Jeanne, do you think he would be proud of me today?"

In her eyes was nothing but calm assurance.

"Your father was always proud of you, Papa. But he could never find the words to tell you."

As I looked at my daughter I didn't doubt her words for a second. Jeanne was right. My father had been proud of me in spite of his hatred. I finally understood this, thousands of miles from the place of my birth, here on the continent of great revolutions, with the image of Che Guevara floating over the city. Why the hell hadn't my father said anything, preferring to take his secret to the grave rather than admit his pride in having a son different from the others, more sensitive, more educated? Ego is the cancer of life, eating away at the heart unless it is controlled.

I rang the bell at number 180, determined to be done with all this, to exorcise once and for all the demons of my childhood, my adolescence, my whole life. A few seconds later, a young woman opened the door. Jeanne served as interpreter.

"Hello, what can I do for you?" she asked with a smile.

"Hello, I am looking for Catherine Schäfer," I said confidently.

"Yes, that's my mother, she's here. Who shall I say it is?"

"Paul Vertune and his family."

"Does she know you?"

"No. But I have known her a long time."

"Ah, very well. Stay here."

She disappeared and then returned a few moments later, beckoning us to enter. We followed the young woman down a corridor, Jeanne and François supporting me. My hands were moist, my heart pounding. The girl in the photograph was here, behind these walls. I had sought her for years, praying that nothing had happened to her.

"My mother is in the garden. She's waiting for you, sir." The young woman clearly sensed the importance of this visit.

Jeanne and François stopped. I looked at my daughter, her face streaked with tears.

"It's up to you now, Papa. Go fulfill your destiny. We are all so proud of you. Aren't we, darling?" she asked François.

"Yes. The little girl from the port is going to find her father. That's the end of the story," he said, beaming with joy.

Moved, I kissed my daughter and my grandson, the young woman silently watching us. I advanced down the corridor, my hands trembling, a little unsteady on my feet, clutching the picture of Catherine Schäfer. Life is a big wheel that carries us aloft to contemplate the panoramic view, then takes us all the way back down again to realize the chance we've had. At that precise moment, as I stepped into the garden, I felt like I was right at the top of the big wheel.

And I saw her. Catherine Schäfer, the little German girl from the photograph, lying on a sun lounger in the shade of a tree. She had grown old but I recognized her immediately. It was definitely she. Everything suddenly coalesced in my mind. I thought of my birth, the priest and the doctor, my father, long Sundays spent digging for clams with my brothers as the smell of the sea filled our nostrils, the washhouse, my schoolmaster, the fields of wheat with their golden ears swaying in the ocean breeze, my mother's perfume, my father's gaze, his coffin descending into the ground, the dark years, the war, the bombs exploding all around, the German officers, Catherine's father dying in front of me, the passing time that never stops, Jean, the drill sergeant, my military service, Frankfurt, Mathilde—my beautiful Mathilde—our first meeting, our long walks along the beach, our awkward teenage kisses, my marriage proposal, Bordeaux, our house, our life together, Jeanne, Martín, the ship, the cyclone, my novel, our happy summer in Andalusia, Mathilde's passing, María, Manuel, life and death— everything they give and take from us. It all mixed together until the emotions were a whirlwind encircling me, the eye of the cyclone of existence, swept by sea winds and breakers. I wept copious tears.

Catherine Schäfer stood up, disconcerted. She had her father's eyes, blue as the ocean, overflowing with kindness. As I walked toward her, the thought struck me that my whole existence was like the phases of the moon, waxing and waning, riddled with craters, which, when I looked closer, wore a wide smile.

EPILOGUE

Kerassel, Morbihan, 2009

It happened in September. During a heat wave, bizarrely, as if the cycle of life had returned to its starting point, the large hands of the clock tired from having revolved for an entire life. One could have sworn that everything was identical, that the natural elements had conspired to meet, as they had eighty years before. The sun beat down on the fields, causing the hard earth to crack, drying out the leaves of plants, which begged for rain. An occasional light breeze off the ocean cooled this furnace a little, caressing our reddened cheeks. Everyone was there, standing by the open grave into which the casket of Paul Vertune, my grandfather, was slowly lowered. The men, well dressed despite the heat, cried openly—not crocodile tears but real ones, heavy with meaning. History blurred the detail of this identical scene, as it always does in its haste. Paul Vertune slipped onward to his destiny.

My mother, Jeanne, sought comfort in her husband's arms. She was an orphan now, the orphan of a deep love that had never known any limits. Paul Vertune's book of life was complete, shelved away in a secret library among billions of other works.

My name is François Lasserre. I'm twenty-nine years old. I am Paul Vertune's grandson. The day my grandfather died, I decided to pick up my pen and write his story.

He lost his memory at the end of his life, because of a dismal disease, an illness that gradually deprived him of his past, ripping out his memories like weeds. Alzheimer's is a strange infirmity, the paradox of an increasing life expectancy, as if the body has let go of the mind's hand on the path of passing time. Soon, Paul Vertune no longer recognized his daughter, or me, or anyone else. He became a shadow on the wall.

We were forced to put him in a retirement home, since he had become quite verbally abusive at times and physically resisted our attempts to wash him, as if his body simply wouldn't accept any violation of his privacy. Sometimes when I went to see him in the park adjoining the home, I watched all those elderly people sitting on their metal chairs, waiting for death like one waits for the subway. I hated the enormous waste of this bottomless well of knowledge and wisdom, which so-called civilized western societies no longer attach much importance to.

Luckily, the retirement home was by the sea, not far from where my grandfather grew up, and he would spend hours watching the sky and the kelp-covered beach, without any comprehension of what he was doing there. Sometimes, when his illness granted him a crack of lucidity, his eyes would suddenly light up. I never knew what he was thinking about in those moments. His words were incomprehensible, no longer conveying the images in his mind. But I'm sure he saw all the people who had counted in his life, all those little heroes we each are in our own way—you who are reading this, sitting on your sofa or on the subway or elsewhere.

Paul Vertune had faith in human nature, which might seem naive in the eyes of those who are full of illusions. He understood from an early age that we all carry good and evil within us, like two suitcases which we fill as we please. My grandfather understood that humanity is built upon a strange contradiction that manipulates us from the shadows. He preferred to nurture the light rather than seek refuge in the darkness.

The priest leaned over my grandfather's grave and made the sign of the cross. People filed past to throw flowers in. Among them I imagined I saw María, Martín, Mathilde, Manuel, Jean, Marc, Jacques, Catherine, and the captain of the ship; they were all there. Delight in his memory filled their tear-streaked faces. Paul Vertune had succeeded not only in life, but also in death.

The ceremony drew to an end and everyone else went home. I remained there, sitting by the grave of the man who had enchanted me with so many stories. I was absorbed in my thoughts, like he used to be. When you're caught inside your head like that, time slips by without waiting for you.

Dusk soon fell on the cemetery, then night. Everything was quiet and still. I began to walk home along the dim path. Looking up, I saw Themoon up in the sky, full yet mournful, having lost its most loyal companion.

ABOUT THE AUTHOR

Photo © 2015 Elodie Tastet

Julien Aranda was born in Bordeaux in 1982. He grew up in southwest France, daydreamed while contemplating the Atlantic Ocean, and read a lot. Nourished by his trips to Latin America, Asia, and the Canary Islands, *Le sourire du clair de lune* (*Seasons of the Moon*) is his first novel. He has recently completed his second novel, *La simplicité des nuages*. Follow him on Facebook at www.facebook.com/julien.aranda.

ABOUT THE TRANSLATOR

Roland Glasser translates literary and genre fiction, as well as art, travel, and assorted nonfiction, from French. His translation of Fiston Mwanza Mujila's *Tram 83* won the Etisalat Prize for Literature 2016 and was long-listed for the Man Booker International Prize and the Best Translated Book Award. He has translated a wide variety of authors, including Anne Cuneo, Martin Page, Marc Pouyet, Ludovic Flamant, Robert Morcet, and Clémentine Beauvais. Roland has contributed articles and essays to the *White Review*, *Asymptote*, *Literary Hub*, *Chimurenga*, *In Other Words*, *Fitzrovia*, and *Bloomsbury*. He has also worked extensively in the performing arts, chiefly as a lighting designer. Having lived in Paris for many years, he is currently based in London.